T0114919

Bitter Leafing Woman

Bitter Leafing Woman

Short Stories

By

Karen King-Aribisala

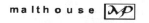

Malthouse Press Limited

Lagos, Benin, Ibadan, Jos, Port-Harcourt, Zaria

© Karen King-Aribisala 2017
First Published 2017
ISBN: 978-978-959-720-8

Published and manufactured in Nigeria by

Malthouse Press Limited
43 Onitana Street, Off Stadium Hotel Road,
Off Western Avenue, Lagos Mainland
E-mail: malthouse_press@yahoo.com
malthouselagos@gmail.com
Website: malthouselagos.com
Tel: +234 802 600 3203

Author's Note

Set in Nigeria, *Bitter Leafing Woman* relates the experiences of Woman as she chews the bitter leaves of patriarchal oppression in a bid to transform them into gender balanced sweetness. Here Woman becomes a symbol of the oppressed; of women and men alike.

The style of writing ranges from plain prose as in *The Edi Kai Ikong War*, magical realism as in *World of the Fat/Thin House*, the social satire of *The Bone Eater*, the densely poetic and symbolic *Broken Plate* and the biblical imbued style of *Bitter Leafing Woman* who finding herself drowning in the soup of gender oppression for forty years attempts to murder her Deacon fiancé.

In this collection we become involved with serious issues of conflicts, which nevertheless we try to treat with sardonic humour and insight.

Karen King-Aribisala
March 2019

Adun Lo N Gbeyin Ewuro
[There is a sweetness that comes only after experiencing bitterness]

- Yoruba proverb

The Stories

Dear Okonkwo

Dear Okonkwo,

How are you? Not exactly the nicest of questions when one considers how you died and that you're actually dead. But we both know your creator, Chinua Achebe, had to yam you out of existence— or rather, that you did the yamming yourself. I'm talking about what happened to you in that world of the novel *Things Fall Apart*. By the way, didn't you know, weren't you aware, that if you existed in a novel with a title like that and you agreed to be the main character, then you would actually fall apart and your society, your world, would fall apart along with you?

What I'm saying, Okonkwo, is that your creator knew the reason why he called his book *Things Fall Apart*. He culled the line from a Yeats poem and it goes like this: "Things fall apart/The centre cannot hold." And you, Okonkwo, with your phallocentric philosophy, as phallic as the yam which was one of the symbols of wealth in your traditional Igbo world, were at the very center, weren't you?

That's part of the reason why I'm writing you this letter. Why indeed did things fall apart in traditional Igbo society, Nigerian society?

I am truly sorry that you are dead, but your life and death taught me a lot about Nigeria. Thus another reason for this letter is to ask your permission to allow me to make known my findings in an investigation I'm conducting on male/female relationships, particularly as they pertain to food and crime in Nigeria. And you, being like the proverbial King Yam, I thought I'd, well, just sort of have a letter chat with you. In any case my telephone is on the blink.

Since you were last here, much has happened in this country. Of course, colonialism and the British colonists have gone for good and Nigeria is an independent nation. But some things are still falling apart. And at the very centre is you. The same old yam and yamming. You see, Okonkwo, your brand of colonialism (I'm talking about male/female relationships) is still going on today. It has to do with male hegemony and patriarchy and with there being little or no female power.

To be blunt, your way is the "Pat-you-into-place-you-female-so-that-you-can-be-my-doormat"   attitude and it is still alive. This attitude is no longer tenable, because the world we live in is getting smaller. You might have heard of the term 'global village'? In any event, whether we like it or not, we are influenced by each other and we all have to be interested in the often terrible lot of women. The need to empower females has led to a burgeoning of Women's Studies. Women are becoming aware of their rights as human beings—although some Nigerians, male and female alike, still cling tenaciously to the view that this interest in

Women's Studies is an importation from the West and doesn't belong here.

These people cite examples of powerful women in Nigeria's history, women like Moremi. They talk about eminent professional women, important market women, and say we have no problem: the African woman is empowered. We're messing ourselves up with Western Feminism, they say, and this is another form of neo-colonialism. And, these people say, that the feminist Kate Millet should stay in the kitchen with her skillet; that the feminist Elaine Showalter will change her opinions when she's led to the altar. That the feminist Florence Howe will soon discover the how of things if she lives in Nigeria. As for Simone de Beauvoir— and any of the other women who wrote and are writing of the lot of Women —well, they wrote with pens and pens are phallic; and if they type their writings, their fingers are phallic too! So these arguments go on and on and this male superior/female inferior thing persists.

Meanwhile, female retaliation crimes are on the rise. Women, Okonkwo, are angry with men and what men have done to them. All this is to explain to you another reason why I'm writing this letter, Okonkwo.

Essentially, as I've hinted before, your dilemma is a yam dilemma. Wealth, power, status, a man's worth in your society was measured by the number of yams a man could harvest and store in his barns. Yam is the male crop, isn't it? Women were left out of this means of acquiring wealth and status in traditional Igbo society which only focused on men. There are exceptions. Your father, for example, preferred to play music day in, day out, instead of being a man like you. But you thought him effeminate, didn't you? And you decided that you wouldn't be like him; that you'd be ever-so-masculine in your approach to him and to life itself!

Then the Europeans came with colonialism and their ideas trying to lord it over your people and over you, especially, the man, Okonkwo. I'm sorry to have to say this, Okonkwo, but you were rather too yam-centred for my taste. Anyway, when the Europeans came, you found yourself in yet another dilemma. First you were troubled by your dad, effeminate, sitting around like a woman enjoying himself playing music and not working, and then, as if that was not bad enough, your manhood was assaulted by the entrance of the Europeans into your world.

You, in your manly way— and I can just imagine it— your bulging biceps, your broad square manly shoulders, and your gun, your phallic yam-gun, participated in the killing of a young boy in your charge whose name was Ikemefuna.

Don't get me wrong. You're a man and men are great. I just feel that you should have sort of balanced your masculine side with your feminine side; but I fear that you had successfully yammed your feminine side out of existence. Don't sulk, Okonkwo. I think that each of us has both feminine and masculine attributes and we've got to reconcile them both with each other, within ourselves. Male and female. Female and male. Not necessarily in either order!

Seriously speaking, Okonkwo, if we don't accommodate our differences then it's going to be for us like it was for you—wahala, trouble, like you've never seen before. I say this, of course, with female humility. To me, your society, as epitomized by you, was male. Yam male. Honestly, I don't know why the Carbohydrate Clan of which yams are a part align themselves with males. Is it a question of their energy, strength, the fact that they are everywhere in the world the providers of starch rigidity upholding the weak? Is it because of their staple-ocity and solidity? My Potato friends--males from the core to the potato peel— for instance, are quite chuffed that there's a potato museum in Ireland devoted to them and their history in that country. That's all well and good. But there's a sinister side to these potatoes. They're rather proud of the nineteenth century Potato Famine in Ireland just because it showed how important they are as potatoes and members of the all-male Carbohydrate Clan.

Anyway, as I was saying, you were given a young boy to look after, the boy I mentioned earlier, Ikemefuna. Ikemefuna would have to be killed at some point because tradition demanded it. But when he stayed with you and your family he was like a son to you; and you grew close to him and you loved him just as if you were his own father and he was your own son. Dare I say it? You loved him like a mother!

The day came to kill Ikemefuna and you were told you didn't have to go with the others and kill him. But you did anyway, basically I think, because you didn't want your feelings, your feminine side, to show. What would people think of an unyammed unmanly Okonkwo? A man has to act like a man and act without fear, doesn't he? Perhaps you should have talked to the male protagonist of D. H. Lawrence in the poem 'Snake' who allowed his female self to be subverted and threw a clumsy log at a snake just because society and the voices in his head said that he should be manly, and go ahead and kill the snake. The two of you would have had something to "Expiate—a pettiness." But I think that poem was written after your time, I'm not sure.

To get back to your *Things Fall Apart* world — Simultaneously the society, just as if it was looking to see what you would do, how to imitate you, was behaving like a stereotyped man striding about and defying the Europeans who were themselves using guns and Bibles — representing the masculine and the feminine sensibilities — to draw the latter to their fold.

I'm not saying we have to be like them. From what I've heard from a Nigerian cook friend who saw Europeans imbibing bloody-looking Napoleon brandy and eating an equally bloody Beef Wellington in memory of some European wars or the other, followed by several helpings of those puddings Dead Man's Leg and Fly Cemetery, their diet is not the best. But we have to know their ways to counter their approach if we're going to succeed in life. On our own terms; which we have, in a way. Let's, for the moment, agree that the Europeans succeeded in the colonial process because they recognized the uncompromising masculine nature of your society and saw how they could conquer us by capitalizing on a weakness in our setup. You might say, Okonkwo, we had a feminine weakness represented by those women who gave birth to twins — a taboo in your culture — and were forced to put them to death in the Evil Forest; those men who were more in touch with their feminine side and who wanted something to fill the hole in their hearts and their souls and went to the Church which you saw only as representing the ways of Europeans; those feminine men. Those people, Okonkwo. O.K., I'm getting a bit passionate here. But how do you think those people felt, as people? Not as women, not as men. Not as Igbo or Yoruba or Nigerian but as people like you and me? They felt like outcasts. That's how they felt. Their world, ruled by the Male-Yam which smothered the feminine dimensions of society, had already fallen apart before the Europeans came.

You thought differently. When you believed your own Okonkwo world had fallen apart because of the European entrance into your life you refused to blame yourself or your society and you committed suicide, didn't you? And in committing suicide you killed not only yourself but also the society which you represent. That's what you did, didn't you, Okonkwo? After such an act, then what happens? Things are 'No longer at ease here in the old dispensation.' That's what. Not that being at ease is a good 'place' to be.

Okonkwo, I don't mean to berate you. I'm sure this letter brings everything back to you and you're probably wishing you had one of your yams to knock me on the head— one of those long big yams you used to store up in your barns. Are you thinking that, Okonkwo? I hope not. I'd be disappointed if you were. It's bad enough that the European in the novel decided to write his account of his stay in Nigeria and entitle it 'The Pacification of the primitive tribes of the Lower Niger,' isn't it?

Anyway I must be off now.

Please could you give me permission to write about my interpretation of Yam and males and everything? I think it might help others who are as yam-inclined as you used to be. Then again it might not. Yam is so hard and you can't eat it unless you first strip it of its skin and then either roast it or boil it or fry it and then probably pound it. Do you know how to prepare pounded yam, Okonkwo? Without it falling apart? I know I've been somewhat harsh but I think you will agree that we have to try to pound the yam together to ensure that it's just the right consistency. Not too soft. Not too hard. So I'm off and away.

Yours who refuses to fall apart but chooses to be a part of,

Goodbye, Okonkwo.

My Sweet Darling Little *Moin-Moin*

To think that his sweet-wording-mouth preceded this downward passage to the nether regioned pit of his body, his stomach.

To think of it...but I did not think of it then...and now this...this consuming darkness...

He called me 'sweetie.' I was sweet, delectable, he said. I made his mouth water, he said. I brought the self of my sweetness to him, he said when he kissed me and held me close in his arms.

And I, caught up in his consuming passion, his bouts of love sickness, which he assured me were becoming more and more protracted, submitted.

He grabbed my hand saying that he would feast his eyes on me; that he was hungry for me, that he would not let go until I agreed to accompany him to his house this very night.

And he held my hand.

I did not wish to refuse him; he had reserved a special table for us at his favourite restaurant.

And I thought that this was the night when he would propose marriage, so that, as he said I would become bone of his bone and flesh of his flesh.

"Say yes! You'll marry me? You'll come home with me?"
"Yes."
"I'm overjoyed. You really are delectable, you know."

"I know."

"Then you must also know that when we're really married…and we're as good as married already…you'll never have to do any housework; you won't ever have to cook again."

I smiled. He was a knowing man. He knew me. And I would never have to cook again. He was a dab hand in the kitchen.

Again his hand covered mine.

"We're going to celebrate my proposal, your acceptance, tonight."

His voice was eager. "We'll have my specialty - *moin-moin* in my flat."

I was overcome by a fit of the giggles. "You've planned this, haven't you? The special dinner here. You knew all along that I'd accept. You decided to have me over at your place for this *moin-moin* snack, didn't you?"

He gazed deep into my eyes. "Have I ever told you how beautiful your eyes are? They are so black."

Then he laughed again.

"You are my darling little *moin-moin*."

"This *moin-moin*…have you cooked it yet?" I asked him.

"No. I want you to see me making it. I want you to see how very much I love you."

But I wasn't ready to leave the restaurant just yet. It was one of the best eating houses in Lagos. Not in terms of the décor, but the food, which was exceptional. It was renowned for its pounded yam, its ọgbọnọ soup and its bush meat.

As if reading my thoughts, he nodded his head in the direction of a fat looking businessman sitting at a table beside us. The man was ogling a heavily made-up woman. She was scantily dressed. They were eating bush meat.

"Bush meat," my man muttered, looking at the woman, looking at the plate, looking at the woman, the bush meat, as some women were called in local parlance... "Delicious, isn't it?" he laughed.

"Not as delicious as your own *moin-moin*, though, I'll bet! Can't we have it here?"

"No. Decidedly no. You wouldn't want to spoil my plans would you?"

Abruptly he rose and I followed him through the dark pressing heat of the room outside to his car. He was silent as we sped our way to his flat; the long deserted streets eaten up, vanishing behind us; and before us the many high scraper buildings reaching down from the sky in passage.

"I can't stomach it," I said.

The remark momentarily jolted him and he took his eyes off the road and looked at me.

"We're nearly there, sweetie. What is it that you can't stomach?"

"Oh, nothing. It's just that this part of Lagos looks so different at night...weird, somehow."

"Nonsense!! Why is my little *moin-moin* talking in that way?"

When we arrived at his flat he went straight to his kitchen to process the beans for the *moin-moin*.

First he emptied the parcels of beans into some cold water. They were creamy in colour, dark eyed, and of a smooth shape—a vegetable comma. They were not the green string beans I preferred, nor the baked beans I sometimes ate with sausages.

He had said he didn't like to see me eat sausages one breakfast morning. He said it made him feel quite queasy to

10

watch me eat sausages; that it quite unmanned him. So I never ate the beans with sausages again. I wanted, especially now, to be everything he wanted me to be and nothing else. Bone of his bone. Flesh of his flesh.

The beans were soaked in cold water until they became soft and their skins could easily be removed.

By that time I was sweating with the kitchen heat, and my skin, especially my little hands which he so loved, were becoming puckered. I removed my dress on his suggestion and then we made a game of it until I was in nothing but my panties. He began to rub the beans together in a washing-like movement in the cold water and their skins slid off and bobbed up in a translucent mass of skins discarded and pale and naked…yes, the beans were strained of their skin clothing and looked naked and bare and unseeing without their dark eyes. Their eyes were thrown away and their clothes were thrown away into the garbage. Then he removed his liquidizer machine from a corner of the kitchen table and he kissed me.

"Be cheerful, sweetie! You'll never have to make *moin-moin* in your life."

He placed the beans in the liquidizer along with onions, peppers and a bit of salt as well as a little water, and ground them until they were transformed into a creamy white paste. He looked at me and tut tutted. "Tut tut," he said. "I must have forgotten something. The mixture is usually a pinkish colour. I know! In honour of your flawless fair complexion, my little *moin-moin*, I'll add some tomato puree!"

I was beginning to feel dizzy, my head pounding with the noise of the liquidizer.

"Are you alright?" he asked.

"Yes, yes…but finish this *moin-moin* quickly…I'm getting a

headache. I need to lie down."

"Just hold on. Hold on; I'll be finished soon. We're nearly done."

As he spoke he opened two tins of tomato puree and scooped the contents into the bean mixture, stirring it until it was the colour of my skin. I touched my face, surprised at its soft moistness. He produced large bundles of leaves and turned the cold water tap on them.

The leaves were dark green flats bigger than my little hands but the same size as his. He then poured the bean mixture into separate leaves, making funnels of each leaf, and folded them into parcels.

By this time I was lying on the kitchen floor but he didn't seem to notice, or, if he did, didn't seem to care. The floor to my eyes at that moment seemed to be the dark green vegetable colour of the green leaves which wrapped around the *moin-moin*; but I knew the floor had been white when I had entered the kitchen earlier, on this, this very night.

I tried to talk, to protest against this transforming—something that was happening to me, but he was too engrossed in what he was doing to notice me.

My arms seemed to have disappeared, so I lay still, biding my time. He would finish soon. He would soon have time for me.

Then I sensed him place the leaf parcels of the bean mixture in a large enamel cooking pot with water. He was steaming them and I knew his concentration would be absolute. I tried to get up from the floor but could not. My legs too, seemed to be gone, now. I had to wait and wait. Wait and wait as I sweated and sweated. It was as if my entire body was one congealing mass; in this kitchen, his kitchen, which was growing increasingly dark.

It was a vegetable dark. The kind of dark in which the beans must have grown before erupting in sunlight and before going down again to dark pot; dark mouth, dark stomach.

The dark down here.

He picked me up in a single scoop. He nibbled my body with the utmost affection.

"My darling little *moin-moin*, how sweet you are and how I do love you!" he whispered.

Those were the last words I heard before I entered this dark place of pressing heat.

And I know, sitting at the very bottom of his stomach in a bean shape of skin, that the moment will come.

The moment will come.

Will come.

A piece of something hits what used to be my head.

What has he eaten now?

It could not be bush meat.

He likes bush meat but he likes me, his little *moin-moin*, much more.

I am his darling sweet little *moin-moin*…so darling, so little, and so very sweet.

The Meat of Leave Me Alone

If Funke had known, only known; had only had a general rough idea of the meaning of the proverb—*Ko si eran to dun to adie afi eran yago (se) fun mi*—which, roughly translated, very roughly translated, means 'No meat is as sweet as chicken, except the meat of leave me alone'—if Funke had only known in translation—authentic or otherwise—what the saying portended—things might have turned out differently. But she didn't know, and so what happened, happened, stumbling her young life into a numbness she would carry to the grave.

And a small confined grave it would be, the dirt particles clinging to the inside shelves of her mind as she heard-watched him; watched-heard him; saw, with wide disbelieving eyes, the animal desire thrusting into her as she screamed "Leave me alone!"

A lecture room where he had first touched timidly her knees under the desk: Leave me alone.

After the lecture he agrees, hands on her hands agrees, that he will leave her alone and that they will be good friends. That.

That she comes from a respectable family. That. That she will not go out with him on a date. She has determined to concentrate on her university studies. A serious relationship will only be considered after she graduates. To all this he, hand-on-her-hands, agrees and says that they will just be good friends.

Though she shines in Language Studies which is their major subject, he has a larger-longer vocabulary. He will assist her in lengthening her vocabulary and he will begin tonight in her flat. And yes, he respects her and he will leave her alone. He respects her and he will not touch her. And his arm is around the arm of her.

She says "I said, I told you. I thought I made it clear. Leave me alone."

He replies that his arm is the arm of a brother and of a fellow student and that he is simply expressing brotherly affection when he puts his arm around her as they look at a book together like brother and sister. Like.

Leave me alone.

And he contemplates this phrase which she has repeated so often it makes him hard. He has to pull his shirt down so that she will not see the effect of Leave Me Alone.

She feels uncomfortable and gets up from the settee, her throat tight, as he doesn't—with all his superior vocabulary knowledge—doesn't seem to know the meaning of Leave Me Alone.

If she could analyze each separate word for him, separately and then together, the words—perhaps, then he would understand.

She would say to him Leave as she has said Leave.

Leave, she would say. Leave means Leave. If you listened to the hard v in it; it would veer you off course, direct you to go. It would make you leave.

But when he hears Leave he thinks of the lulling ease of a leaf, lush-green, virgin, falling, falling from a stem to which the leaf had clung, falling with ease.

She would, if she could talk to him, she would talk of Me. Her self. Me which is hers and hers alone. Me. Leave Me.

But when he hears Me he thinks of himself, his own me. His-me. And being vocabularly elongated, he translates in his inner self his *ko si eran to dun to adie afi eran yago (se) fun mi* into another language.

The meaning, roughly, will soon be made clear.

Alone. She want-needs to be alone; to be the all that is in all and the one that is all-one and not to be in the aloneness she feels.

And he thinks "I've got her alone, all to myself, alone. When she tells me she wants to be alone she wants the one that is me. The all that is me inside her when she says 'Leave Me Alone."

She does not. She refuses to join together the words of the phrase. She says them separately. "Leave" she says. "Me" she says. "Alone" she says. Leave Me Alone.

And he pulls his shirt down more as she says "It's getting late. I have an eight o'clock lecture tomorrow."

"And so do I. Can I have a drink? Got any chicken?"

Leave Me Alone.

"Chicken?"

"Can I have some coffee, tea? I know you've got some in your kitchen."

"And then you really must go," she replies, feeling his eye-watching, not seeing that he has abandoned the struggle with his shirt.

And when she returns with mugs of coffee in both hands and sees the eyes of him, she is afraid of an unseen urge which unabashedly rises in him and is rising as.

As he knocks down the mugs which shatter to the floor,

the hot coffee scalding her bare legs and staining her clothing with a stain which will stain her in her very grave.

The insides of her stained.

As he rips her dress. As. Leave Me Alone is a phrase which does not help. The words do not assist. They goad him on, throw her to the floor; cause thrusting-jerk-of-spasm-jerk in her. The shelves of her mind quick-filling with dirt. A lone woman on the floor with the hurting knowledge that he will never leave her alone.

And then he leaves her alone.

She rushes to her bathroom and a surge of sickness leaves her in a vomiting bile of filth and she enters the shower, cold water drenching her skin. She has lost her skin. She rubs with a towel what she had considered to be her skin. Her me-skin. And.

And at the police station she reports the incident to a policeman, telling of a man who would not leave her alone.

The policeman hears "Leave Me Alone."

Is goaded on and in by the phrase of "Leave Me Alone."

The policeman presses her back to the floor.

Her back pressed against the floor, on the floor.

The floor is a coffined grave, her mind quick-filling with dirt.

Leave.

Me.

Alone.

Purification

"It's about time to leave," he muttered, glancing at the large clock on the mantle-piece. Beside the clock were photographs of him, of her; of the two of them as a couple, a married couple of some two years.

Yes. It was time to leave.

The night darkened inside the room. The electricity and the generator that was used to give them light had both failed. They had to rely on candles to see the food on the plates on the dining table.

The food. He picked up his napkin, which she had washed and starched and ironed, and folding it so that it resembled an elongated length of rigid cloth, dabbed at his lips which were not soiled with the red palm oil sauce of the stew. Dab dab. He dabbed his lips. He pulled the fork and the knife together on his plate so that the metal scraped-steeled her insides as they closed. The fork and the knife. He hunched his shoulders looking as one bemused at the action of pulling fork and knife together on a plate. Then seeming to think more of it, studiously prized them apart as if they were heavy instruments.

As if they were not fork and knife.

He had prepared the meal this night. Ever since they had been married he had insisted on cooking their food for five, six, or seven days every month. Eating at restaurants, he had told her, was a risk he was not prepared to take. The food might have been cooked by an unclean woman. And in his part of

Nigeria, custom forbade it. She should understand.

Why, if a man had more than one wife, which was usually the case—then he would send the unclean wife to an outhouse at her unclean time of the month. She was not allowed to cook for him. His other wife would do the cooking until her own unclean time came. Came. Came. She didn't want a polluted husband, did she?

Fortunately she was regular and he did not have to check the calendar for the dates of each month when it happened. But he had drawn circles in red crayon around the figures; the dates of the days of the months of the years during which they had been married. He drew the circles around those days all the same. And he drew them clearly.

"Have you brought them out from the store and packaged them in plastic bags as I told you? The last time . . ."

She shuddered. The last time.

"I'll just clear up these dishes and wash them before we go. Is that alright?"

He nodded. "Be quick about it. But you haven't answered my question. Did you package them properly?"

The sound of clattering plates piled one on top of the other. The tinny din of forks and knives. The language of the fork. The language of the knife. The fork and the knife. He asked her again if she had packaged them as he had said she should.

Pack. Packaged. "I've actually put everything into one of my suitcases, the small one, you know, the travelling one. And I have the bag."

"Good idea. I should have thought of that myself."

She took the stack of plates, the cutlery, into the kitchen. He followed, holding an empty tray in his hands. "I forgot to ask you if you . . . did you buy any of those air-freshener things? The last time . . ."

Her hand grasped the sponge tightly, the knuckles protruding like raw nubs of bone until she felt they would erupt and jump through her skin and she would have no hands left to hold the suitcase or open the front door and leave with him into another night.

"Air freshener? No!" She dried her hands. "But I could bring along some cologne if you like."

"If I like?"

His voice arched above her. She hastily placed the last of the dishes in the rack, and then moving from the sink to the kitchen wall, again dried her hands with a cloth which hung from a nail. The action was too hasty. The nail pierced her hand and the daub of blood which he saw even in the dark moonlit kitchen seemed to ignite him.

"If I like?"

He exaggerated the words.

"If . . . I . . . like? Let's get this straight. I'm helping you out. Do you think I enjoy having to do the cooking every month for five, sometimes seven days? Do you think I like having to leave my house in the middle of the night every blasted month?"

Month, month. Think, think. She had been thinking of the unclean and the need for purification. All these months she had been thinking. The halt, the sober brevity of her "Thank you" gave him pause.

"I'm off to change my clothes and then we'll go, O.K.?"

She saw the striding length of his trousered legs as they scissored their way out of the kitchen. He would turn at the corner of the living room wall and then climb up the stairs to the upper floor of the house where the bedrooms were. She knew without seeing him return that he would be dressed in his oldest washed out *sokoto* and *dansiki*; the outfit he always wore on these occasions. He would hoist his bag onto their bed and into it dump a pair of rubber gloves, his torch, matches, and a bottle of petrol which he kept in the corner of the wardrobe.

She dragged her feet to the dining room. She felt very, very tired. But then she was used to feeling like this during these periods. Her own bags had been packed earlier in the day when there was no one around to see. The servant had been asked to stay away from the house. Had left with a mixture of sadness and mischief in her eyes for Madam. She was certain the servant knew what they did, and what they were about to do.

Probably the whole village knew.

"Ready, then?" His voice was cheerful.

"You'll carry your own bags, won't you? By the way, where are they?"

She gestured to the front door.

"Why on earth did you put the bags there? This is getting beyond me."

The words reeled on. Spittle formed at the edges of his mouth as it always did whenever he had one of his angry bursts of temper.

"I have to cook for us every month and then . . . and then . . . what if someone were to enter the house and see those bags? What would they think of you?"

She sighed, dropping deep into an armchair, her attention drawn to the clock on the mantle-piece. The photographs of him, of her, of the two of them. She thought of knives.

He said "Just after midnight. Let's go."

At the door, he half-turned to look at her.

"Why did you say you had to have two bags?"

"Things have been quite heavy for me this month."

"I'll say they have," he said, jangling his car-keys, opening the door, and walking out onto the patio, his boots crunching on the driveway. Jangling his keys. Keys on keys. Jangle. Fork and knife. Jangle. Knife.

"Let's get this over with. I'm tired with all the cooking I've had to do this week. I've found a new place."

She wasn't listening. She scanned the exterior of the house and the night nestling around it. Theirs was the largest house in the village. In the distance squat huts emitted fumes of smoke and she could only guess at the families, the husbands and wives sitting around their evening meals. No. It was too late for that. Much too late. They would be sleeping. Too late for that, too.

His voice jarred her ears alive.

"I've chosen a place two kilometres from here . . . No one lives around there. Nobody will see us."

Sitting in the backseat of the car she watched him go through the contents of his bag, his tones a steady drone.

"That's it: torchlight, petrol, matches, gloves. I take it you've brought the cologne?"

But she was listening to the night with its night hours ticking by. The night with its noises and its noised silence. She pushed her head out of the window and looking up saw a slither of moon behind a fuzz-white waste of clouds which should have been there in the daytime—but it was night-time.

"What are you doing?" he asked, and he turned the ignition key, once, twice, before the engine rasped.

"I was watching the moon," she said. And what she did not say filled her heart. That the moon should have shone round-white-egged and that it should not have split with moon-sorrow tears trickling down her face exposing yolk-specked-red as her body felt; was feeling.

He was driving slowly, his hands on the steering. "Can't think why I didn't smell it the moment I came into the house. It's a good thing, though," he reflected, looking at her in the mirror, "or else I would have felt too unclean to do the cooking and we wouldn't have had anything to eat tonight."

And she thought of the way he had parted fork and knife on his plate.

Fork and knife. Fork. Knife. He began to whistle as he drove past the huddled huts of the village. He whistled. Makeshift trestle tables lined one side of the road. People jostled, their figures silhouetted in the lantern light; and she could dimly make out heaps of bread bloated white, one loaf on top of the other. Tins of milk formed pyramids; kola nuts cramped their in-held bitterness in globular shapes and fish roasted and slime-varnished, sprawled on trays, their tails in their mouths in round circles of fish. And she wondered at the effort it must have taken to ensure that the long fish became round-circled-round, like a moon; like an egg.

"You could have bought some food here," she ventured, then bit her lip as anger leapt into his accelerated feet, the car racing so quickly that pedestrians had to jump out of his path. A woman selling fish raised her fist at him; and they sped past vast tracts of land and rubbish merged into a wide waste of filth. She closed her eyes.

When she opened her eyes and the eyes of her thoughts, they had reached, as he had earlier said, an abandoned area.

In Mushin, one of the worst slums she had ever come across in Lagos, she had seen rubbish piled high as houses. Wastelands of it. People lived twenty to a room in spaces smaller than her bathroom. Gutters solid with stagnant water and discarded refuse formed thick still carpets around and between the houses. This place was worse. Much worse.

"You can get out. And you needn't make a face. You're a woman. You know intimately about this." His hands spread out.

"Well get a move on. Burn the damn things!"

"I..I...can't. I have a pain in my stomach, I—" she stammered. Roughly, he extricated himself from his position behind the wheel, got out of the car, pulled on his rubber gloves, removed the plastic bag from the boot, and walking rapidly to the nearest heap of rubbish carefully placed it at the very top. Her plastic bag. It resembled a female body with lumps of breasts and belly and its own lump of head tied at the neck with a cord ready for suttee burial, where the plastic body would be burned on the funeral pyre and join in death the death of her husband. She had seen a film once. It took place in India and the widow was placed on a funeral pyre to join her dead husband. And she wondered then and now at the waste of it; of life; of conceptions; the waste; of plastic bags containing her sanitary napkins with their soiled waste.

She laughed.

"What are you doing?" he shouted, taking off his gloves; he wanted to set the plastic bag alight. "I thought you said your stomach was hurting? And what about the napkins in your suitcase?"

She manoeuvred herself into the front seat of the car and she laughed. She was surprised she could laugh. She laughed again just to hear the sound of it from her mouth. Her own mouth. Her very own mouth with which she laughed.

"Be quiet! There might be people around!"

"And these people might be women and they might have periods; they might be menstruating. How horrible!"

She was laughing and laughing.

"Come over here, woman! Right now!—and set this thing alight. The stench is killing me. I'm having difficulty setting— get out! You're obviously not as sick as you claim to be during your periods. Get out of the car!"

A pause.

"I'm a man. I'm not supposed to even get close to the damn things—to see them, even. You're making me unclean, woman!"

Even, even.

He was advancing in long scissored strides; but she had already turned the ignition key. The car raced past him.

The waste.

Another Life/Another's Life

It is the beauty of the kill that excites. The way the strings of the heart pull tight in concentration at the sight of the victim. Small children know this.

They know the thrill, the inward pleasure of seen suffering, seen death, when with sling-shots tight in hand, they circle the forbidden bird.

The elastic is pulled forwards, the pebble is fixed to the far end of the elastic. The sling shot is pulled back, back and the pebble is catapulted forward. The pebble hits the bird-feathered flesh of the bird. Its beak stutters the ground. The bird flaps its wings once, twice. The bird lies dead on the ground.

Perhaps there is a small ounce of blood on the body of the bird where the pebble struck. Perhaps not. But the bird is dead, struck- stricken into silence as their little child feet glide past with living soles treading with a new power . . . a new power denied their child-adult-directed- lives.

And they pocket their sling-shots, their catapults; and so armed, they fly and soar new sky-heights; returning to their genteel Ikoyi homes with their green grass sprawl of gardens and sturdy sophisticated trees which laze with leaves brushing the sky and which surround large houses of white and pale-cream-- looking on as the trees look on at what the children have done to another life. These children do not care; even when scolded they do not care. They do not care because they have found a killing power that is in their hands and they can pocket it along with their sling-shots for later use on this bird and on that.

At first I was silenced by their look of contentment before anger surged.

"You wicked children! You shouldn't do that. The bird hasn't done you anything. Birds are living creatures too."

A scamper of little child feet and a lingering trail of giggles as I stroke the poor dead bird. I pick up the sling-shot. It is made from two twigs bound with elastic. Doubtless another would be made. But at least this particular sling-shot would not murder another life . . .

Another life . . . she, too, my one-time friend, said she wanted and needed another life. She said her marriage had ended .She said the romance in her marriage had gradually fizzled away. Her husband no longer called her darling, dear; no longer caressed her cheek nor whispered endearments, no longer held her hand. She said she yearned for flowers, a single rose bought for her alone and given to her alone from him. She wanted kisses and endless love making. She wanted to capture him again, enthral him as she had when they had first met.

And so she'd decided to have an affair. An intensely romantic affair...

The man would give her boxes of chocolates and kisses and curvy bottles of sweet white wine. She wanted a man who would kiss her knees and murmur into her hair and tell her only she mattered in the whole wide world. She wanted it and craved it with her entire being all the way down to her exquisite knees. She said this man of the would-be affair had told her that she had exquisite knees. That's what she said.

She said the rest she could handle. One night of love was all she wanted with this man. Then she would return to her husband and give him—she said, giggling a trail of giggles—the benefit of her experience. And the wanting grew with a greed which consumed even those exquisite knees. She needed help. Mine. A place had to be chosen for the affair. A hotel, she said, had too much of a commercial ambience.

"It's the money you know, paying to stay at an hotel—I'd feel used."

"Whatever, but you can't use my place. I don't feel right about it."

"That's not the point. You see, the moment money changes hands I'd feel like some sort of prostitute."

"Well, you would be as you say, some sort of prostitute."

"Don't get on your high horse with me!"

Idly she removed a flower from the vase before her and began to pull at the petals one by one.

"But what would your husband say?"

"Say? My husband? He doesn't have to know. He will not know, I promise. I couldn't betray our friendship. Besides, he doesn't even know I exist. He doesn't care. I thought I'd explained all that to you."

"You did explain. But he would be hurt. Even if he doesn't know about the affair you're planning; even if he doesn't love you he'd be hurt."

She was becoming more petulant and brandished the now petal-less stem in her hand.

"It'll just be for one night" she coaxed.

"Why a night, why not a day, why not a month?"

"Oh you do go on. Why, I thought you understood me."

"I'm not sure that I do. Tell me again," I said, resisting the impulse to smack the once again busy hand. She was tearing the stem to shreds.

"I want to be loved by this man for a night—to live again. I want some romance."

"And then what?"

"Then, oh, I don't know . . . I'll treasure the memory."

"So you want to, to commit adultery, so you can feel romantic?"

"I should never have said anything to you. We are best friends. You know how I've been suffering—If for nothing else do it for me, for us in the name of friendship."

It was true she had grown thin in the last few years, her large Ikoyi house with its equally large gardens plumb in the most expensive area of Lagos was filled with the wandering ghost of her past self and I told her, "I just want to make sure you know the ramifications of what you intend to do."

"Ouch! I'm not talking buildings. It's really quite simple. I want him for a night and the only place I can think of is your place. Please, in the name of our friendship…"

Even if I did succumb to her request which I knew I would—how could I explain her? She could charm an ogre—and perhaps against my better judgment we had been friends for simply ages and I had always helped her out of one scrape or the other . . . and she really had grown thin and so very sad . . . but I had to give her a hard time . . . and she was my best friend . . . and . . . .

"Why, what's so special about my place?"

"Well, you're my best friend, for one, at the moment,

and, and—you're alone at the moment, and I really think I'll be able to make my husband more romantic after this, he'll love me more, and it would be so very romantic of you."

She leaned back in a chair, crossed her legs and sucked her thumb like a child. She had a habit of doing that and her husband, she said, liked it because it spoke of her childlike innocence. The very first time they had made love, well, it had been catapulted into being by this sucking of her thumb after which she sucked each individual finger on his hands; and then seeing his wondering eyes, she pulled off his shoes and his socks, just pulled them off in single backward movements she said, and she said that she began to suck each of his toes. Weird, I know, but it worked. He was smitten. He was, she said, beside himself at this stage, and proposed soon after. And later still, one of those fingers which she had herself sucked sported a wedding band.

"Does this man you intend to have an affair with, go in for this sucking thing?"

"Do be serious!"

"Does he?"

"As a matter of fact, yes. I sucked my thumb at a very important dinner which he attended and he was enchanted."

"You're impossible," I told her. "Will tomorrow be alright?"

"Tomorrow? Oh, you are an utter darling!"

She immediately began planning what she would wear—subdued, deliberately sexy clothing, or 'little girl,' were the choices laid before me.

"Little girl, I think, with a dash of adulthood thrown in if you think you can manage it."

"You are my very bestest friend," she enthused. "I'll wear

a kind of pinafore and tie my hair up in bunches; and I think blue knickers would do well. I can still get into my old school uniform you know!"

"Blue knickers? Knickers? You mean you saved your school panties as well as your school uniform?"

And she giggled rushing out of the house, presumably to contact the selected man for the proposed affair.

* * *

With an irony I did not see at the time I spent the following night in an hotel, the bill paid for by her in the name of our friendship. But she didn't come to see me until a day or so after the affair and when she did come she was somewhat—I don't' know—she looked rather serious for one who had after all gotten what she'd wanted, a night of fire with a secret lover so that she could , as she said, "live again."

"How did it go?"

"Need you ask? Can't you see? It was marvellous. Of course I shan't see him again."

Characteristically, she began to suck her thumb.

"Oh, by the way," she asked "Why did you leave a sling-shot on the bed?"

"I didn't."

"Yes you did."

She produced the sling-shot which I had earlier confiscated from the little child killers of that bird. I must have left it on my bed before going to the hotel.

"My lover didn't like the sling-shot. In fact he got quite upset about it. He said it reminded him of when he saw his boyhood friends kill birds . . . when he was a boy . . . and that he didn't like to remember."

She was pouting.

"So?"

"So he didn't like the sling-shot and it kind of spoilt things. He said he didn't like to think of me with a sling-shot and I told him it wasn't mine. It didn't belong to me."

"Where is the sling-shot? I meant to throw it away—"

She produced it from the interior of her caftan and, instead of giving it to me, pocketed it again.

"Can I have that sling-shot please?"

"No you cannot have the sling-shot. I want to keep it as a kind of memento even though—"

"Anyway, how do you think it will be with your husband now?" I asked as carefully as I could.

"Oh, all right, I suppose. He's started complaining about me sucking my thumb though, and he said he never liked to see me sucking my thumb and he said I was a liar and all sorts of things!"

"But why?"

She turned her back to me before replying. She walked with tight steps, her body taut, to the window of the room and back again and then she faced me.

"I had to tell him about it, the affair, you know. . .I had to tell him and . . . that I used your place. You do understand don't you?"

"You told your husband? How could you do that to me? Why?"

"I mean I couldn't lie to him, he is after all my husband, and he's also my best friend. My very bestest friend. I felt I should tell him, he is my husband after all. Look if he questions you about it, just listen. I had to tell him you helped me to set things up and that we did it in your house.

32

When I was looking happy and glowing after the um, affair—like he said—and he asked me 'how come,' I had to tell him the truth, you see."

"Yes, I did help you, didn't I? As I recall, in the name of our friendship."

"Oh come on. Don't look like that. Don't be angry with me! He *is* my husband."

"He is your husband," I repeated bitterly.

"Poor dear! When I told him—and especially about your part in the thing—he looked so wounded. Poor dear! His hands kind of flapped about and he pursed those beautiful lips of his and he sort of gasped and then he just sort of curled up on the bed. I have never seen him like that, you know . . . so absolutely wounded. It was like, it was like he seemed so small and well honestly I have to tell you . . . it was so exciting . . . I've been feeling alive ever since I told him about the affair and about your hand in it for some reason. It's odd isn't it, but he was perfectly irresistible!"

"Irresistible?"

"Perfectly irresistible."

The *Edi Kai Ikong* War

Simi was a practical woman. But when her husband's new wife screamed screams of pleasure in his hut, the sound rivalling successfully the other sounds of the night, it hurt her. She swallowed. Tried to maintain her composure as the new woman strutted and preened herself in their husband's compound. Tall, elegant, plump—it was no wonder that her husband had fallen for this woman's charms.

The children seemed to be especially enchanted. They had coaxed her to sit down. They were smoothing oil over the woman's arms and legs, and the woman had even pulled down her wrapper exposing her midriff and the beads around her belly; and to Simi it seemed that the very beads jingling around the woman's waist adored their owner, were engrafted to their owner. And that those beads with their eye bead after malice; after malice eye bead, hated her. Simi. The first wife. The senior wife.

The woman arched her long neck and shouted at a servant. "You had better keep this compound clean oh! My husband has to have a decent place to live in!"

Brooms. The servants sweeping vigorously the already clean compound which Simi, rising at dawn, had herself swept. What was to be done? Two months of marriage had still not shown their husband that this second wife was nothing but a greedy, grasping woman who wanted to be first wife and lord it over everyone; Simi, the children and her unwitting husband.

That husband of their youth and the youth of their together dreams. With her by his side he had fulfilled his dreams. She selling produce from the farm; selling knick knacks with one, two, three babies on her back until—

The woman addressed her: "My senior wife, I see you are relaxing."

"I'm just about to prepare our husband's meal—*amala* and *ewedu*,"

"No need for that. Last night—" the woman grinned, exposing a gap between her two front teeth—a feature of beauty much admired in the area-- "No need my senior wife. No need for you to trouble yourself. You are old. You need some rest. Our husband told me that I will always be the one to cook every meal for him. He has been telling me that from the day I entered this compound."

"He said that?" inquired Simi. Had her husband lost his senses to entrust this, this woman to such an extent that he would go against tradition to—to please his new wife?

Before she could respond, both women were surprised to see their husband approaching. In spite of the night's activities, at the sight of his new wife, he appeared discomfited. "I've been shouting for someone to fetch me water but the servants, I see, are sweeping the compound. Do not let this happen again."

The young woman prostrated before him, her waist beads and her wrapper falling to the ground.

"Ah! My wife, you will tire me all over again."

He pulled her up and took her to his hut and Simi averted her eyes. Let them do whatever they wanted to do in her husband's hut. She would cook the meal she had planned for him, whatever that upstart had said. Maybe she should cook something different. Not *amala* and *ewedu*. He was too accustomed to it. She had a sneaking suspicion that this new wife from Calabar had prepared *edi kai ikong* for her husband on one of his visits to the region, and that she was still doing so. That particular soup was famed throughout Nigeria. Any woman who cooked it and gave it to a man would enslave him forever.

It was time to do battle. Simi herself would cook *edi kai ikong*. The ingredients for the soup could not be obtained easily but for the sake of her marriage, to restore her husband's affections to her as first wife, she must act quickly and act now.

In broad daylight. She could hear them. In broad daylight. Her husband had no shame. Nor had the woman. The woman had no shame. She, Simi, would make the *edi kai ikong*. She and her husband were Yoruba and she was not from Calabar. She had never cooked *edi kai ikong*. But she would fight.

"Akon!" she called a servant.

"Yes?"

That was another thing. Since the second's wife entrance into her life, the servants, especially this Akon, showed her no respect.

He didn't even want to address her as Ma. She would not reprimand him. Not now...not yet.

"Akon, you are from Calabar!"

"Yes."

"I want you to go to market now and get all the ingredients for *edi kai ikong* soup."

"But —"

"Go!" shouted Simi. "You'll find some money for transport over there."

Let him fetch it himself. When he had gone she felt

perhaps it was not such a good idea to send Akon to the market. He might have gotten wind of her intentions. And if he knew what she was up to he, a Calabar man, wouldn't want her, a Yoruba, to be the victor in this *edi kai ikong* war. He would want his new mistress—

What if he returned without a certain particular ingredient, something very crucial? She knew some of the things the soup should contain: periwinkles, crabs, fresh fish, stock fish, water leaf and another leaf whose name she could not remember. She should have watched that second wife preparing it.

Time was passing and Akon—where was he? She would cook *amala* and *ewedu*. That was her husband's favourite dish and had always been ever since she had met him when her family had given her to him as wife. Senior wife. First wife. Wife who had given birth to his three children...who had suffered along with him...until he was the man he is today.

At this very moment, the second wife and their husband had probably come to the end of whatever they were doing and that *edi kai ikong* of a woman had, by now, most likely made their husband's dinner.

Ah! But maybe *edi kai ikong* was all that woman was good for and nothing else. It was shocking that a man could lose his senses because of what a woman, that woman, fed him. The *ewedu*, it tasted good. The *amala* was turned in the pot, its dark mound of cassava flour having been stirred in hot water. The soup was ready. It contained that special stock fish which she had bought on her last trip to the market just two months ago when he had returned, her own husband, from Calabar with the produce of his trade and his new wife simpering coyly around the edges of his *agbada* like so much beaded embroidery. That was the day she bought the stockfish.

She had had no prior warning about this marriage—and apparently, neither had he. The new wife had even had the gall to announce how she had caught—she said "caught." How she had caught their husband with the famed *edi kai ikong*.

Akon still hadn't returned. Her husband ate precisely on the dot at six in the evening. At five minutes to six, the *amala* and *ewedu*; everything was ready. Simi placed the calabashes of food in a basket and covered their steaming richness with a cloth.

Tonight she would personally serve her husband.

Even if that woman's beads jiggled or if the two of them, he and she, were—! She banished the thought, and putting the basket of food on her head, made her way to her husband's hut. For two whole months she had not felt his touch. She had not prepared a single meal for him because of that woman.

Tonight was war, *edi kai ikong* or not. She lowered her head and went into the hut. Her husband and his new wife were there and she was setting out calabashes of *edi kai ikong* and *foo foo* before him and chattering endlessly. She ignored Simi's entrance and Simi's heart began to pound. What if…What if her husband spurned his favourite soup and *amala* and *ewedu*!

And when her husband grasped his second wife's waist and her beads fell to the ground, Simi's heart sank. He washed his hands in a bowl of water and Simi felt her knees shaking. "My senior wife," he said, "I have been waiting for this soup with *amala* and *ewedu* for two whole months, yet you have refused to come to my hut to give it to me! I told my second wife to inform you of this and yet you have refused to come and serve me until now. At last you have come. I was beginning to wonder whether the many struggles we shared together were for nothing."

"But I thought you, you loved *edi kai ikong* and—"

"*Edi kai ikong* is delicious," said her husband agreeably.

He motioned to the junior wife…

"My dear, I'm old and very tired. Leave me and my senior wife and think on these words: *Obe ti basale ki I je iyaale ki*. I see you haven't learnt to speak Yoruba yet so I'll translate.

"Better still, Simi, you tell her."

Simi felt pity for her co-wife but said the words nonetheless.

"The soup which the husband doesn't take, the senior wife doesn't prepare it."

The young woman stood rooted to the spot. Simi explained further.

"The most senior wife cooks the soup of the husband because she is the most trusted and genuine love. She knew the man when he was nothing, you see."

The young woman tied her wrapper, loosened it, then re-tied it. Simi, in spite of her hurt, felt sorry for this second wife and sorry for herself that she had had to wage war with this fellow woman over this man with *edi kai ikong*, with *amala*, *ewedu* and their husband's favourite soup—with anything, when it might have been so different.

But Simi was a practical woman. Stifling her remorse and any ideals she might have cherished, she went to war…

"Second wife, junior wife, who is such an expert with *edi kai ikong*, make sure you pick up those waist beads of yours before you retire to your hut. You wouldn't want our husband to slip and fall, would you?"

The Law of the Black Berry

When first I saw her, first; she was a parody of the black-beautied berry of which she spoke. And when she spoke of it with such feeling I died with a within-me-dying for her as one who had taken part as she had been taken apart from the very earth dark-loaming-soiled and made to be what she was not, out of season and out of growing time; of fruition time. Out of a time, untimely plucked. For eating.

She spoke of the eating of the black berry born on her very own tree. A fruit famed for its luscious shine of plump rounding flesh-covering-seed.

"He knew what he was doing. Papa's best friend had married me even as my mother was giving birth to her fifth child."

"Surely you exaggerate?" I prompted.

She shook her braids.

"And Papa's best friend . . ."

"You mean your husband?"

"Yes, my husband. He could not wait as tradition, our culture demands, for me to reach the age of puberty before he...he had . . ."

"Sexual relations?"

She trembled like the child she was.

"I promise not to interrupt," I said.

It had taken her a long time to even agree to be

interviewed. In the end she had accepted. She said she did not want her sisters, any young girl, to suffer the same pain; the same fate as she had.

She, like the black berry which the he of her husband had called her, was a special fruit of woman with her dark black shiny skin, luminous in sheen.

The seed is small and it is placed in a hole in the earth.

"He, my husband I mean, sent his most senior wife to fetch me. I was playing with my baby brother and my senior wife said our husband had need of me. I thought that he wanted me to sit on his lap and tell me a story as he often did. I would sit on his lap and he was just like my Papa. Then his eyes would redden after he finished the story and he would shout for my senior wife to take me away. This time it was different."

After the seed of the black berry is put in the soil it is not plucked or eaten. The law of the black berry demands a waiting for nurturing; for growth before it can be eaten.

"He said he had a special story to tell me; one that I had never heard before and I was happy. Like the other times, I sat in his lap and he told me a story."

Water is needed for the black berry to grow. If, as often happens in these arid regions where dust is King and desert is King, the water refuses to appear, there is a waiting and sometimes a walking to the well to fetch the water from the well with a water pot from the well; and after lowering the pot into the well of water there is more walking to the black berry spot where the seed is planted and it is carefully watered.

"The story he told me that day I cannot remember. I felt a hardness under me as I was sitting on his lap and I saw the red eyes of my husband and I expected him to shout to my senior wife to come and get me. I saw him remove his gown and he hurt the inside of me and I cried and my tears were wet on my face."

In the planting of the black berry there is need of sun which does not come when you call it; is not switched on like an electric lamp, bulb with a switch to the finger readiness of your hand.

Sometimes the sun comes and sometimes it does not. But when it comes it moves-sun-moves into the earth in waiting for growth.

Just waiting. Waiting for growth.

"I was ten. Ten years old."

Ten is long in the life of the black berry tree. It is not long in the life of a woman, a girl. In time it is not long. She has, this girl, not ripened, even yet. The water of rain and of well and the heat of the sun have need of more time to ripen her as she fidgets with the hem of her dress. Unsure still of what has taken place and why, after giving birth to her child she makes journeys hitherto and back to relieve herself of untimely water; the water from a birth from which she has departed and the water which she cannot control as he, her husband had sought and did; had sought to partake of and did. Control her growth and did.

This girl-woman-child has need of tending.

The black berry must be cared for and nursed as it rises from the earth of its home pushing its tendrils up for air, its leaves to breathe in as it grows on the vine and before it ripens and is plucked and is eaten.

"I must excuse myself."

Another water-relief-walk as she runs at the bidding of a body uncontrolled.

She is holding her face when she resumes her seat beside me on the mat.

"How are things with you now? I promise I shall do everything I can to change the laws of child marriage in this state—everywhere—I'll campaign and get others to join me. It is intolerable, wrong; what you've been forced to go through."

She is not the only one. There are many young girls such as herself; black-berry-treed, untimely plucked in need of right soil, right water, right sun; in need. In need of growth.

Before plucking. In need.

"Let us go. I want to show you the black berry tree. It has delicious fruit and I would like to give you some as a present before you leave us."

"I do hope you won't get into trouble for talking with me . . . with your husband . . . he won't harm you further will he?"

"It is my husband who suggested that I give you presents of black berries before you leave. He said that I must take you to the black berry tree and show you the tree."

The tree. We go to this black berry tree. The tree. Not only is it stripped bare of fruit, but a someone – on coming closer I can see that a someone has ripped it from the earth in which it nurtured stood; has buried it upsided-down-down-sided-down as if in violation of some natural law, and its roots dirtied with soil shoot up scratching the air.

Her hands to her yell of mouth; she cannot with-hold the water of her eyes; those waters and other waters.

And on the face of her husband who appears; a smile which mocks the law of the black berry tree which he has planted upsided-down-upsided down.

World of the Fat-Thin House

Shock on the old woman's face.

When Ekaete should have been eating food like pounded yam and edi kai ikong like the other girls in the fattening house, when she should have been feeding, getting nice and plump to fatten the eyes of the prospective husbands at the marriage dance on the morrow, what was Ekaete doing? She was eating. And she was eating American News.

"Ekaete, you're not eating selected pages of *The National Enquirer* are you, not again?"

Ekaete was indeed munching some selected pages of an old copy of *The National Enquirer*. She had chosen this magazine to eat because it had 'enquirer' on its front and she was an enquiring sort of girl, Ekaete.

In a leisured manner she munched on Monica's misery. It was a story about what happened to the infamous famous Monica Lewinsky who had an affair with President Clinton of America. He lied about the affair on national TV when the nation wanted to know something about their President's diet...If he was eating wholesome family food at home with his wife Hillary or if he wasn't. He said Monica lied about their affair. Then he said she didn't lie. It was true. He had had an affair. Monica became miserable and it affected her diet. She wasn't miserable because the affair was exposed to America and the world. She was miserable because she was believed to have ratted on the President of the United States, the greatest, most powerful nation of the world. How could she have been so unthinkingly treacherous as to reveal that the President of the United States was a man who got a bit peckish sometimes for food on the side ? The article said Monica said, "Food is my only friend . . . No man will have me . . . They're trying to kill me." In effect Monica had Lewinskied herself good and proper since no man would risk attaching himself to this Monica.

Ekaete paused in her eating then decided to eat page twenty-four which was still going on about Monica's diet. Monica said, "My only solace comes from eating. Food is now my aphrodisiac and my tranquilizer. But I'm probably eating myself to death!"

That's the painful lament of a shattered Monica Lewinsky, who's packed on 50 pounds since the sexgate scandal erupted. Monica said, "I feel like an animal in a cage. All I do is pace around each day, waiting and wondering when I'm going to be let out. Nut cases have sent death threats or left messages, calling me a traitor, a spy on a mission to destroy the country. Even my parents have received death threats." She'll order a large pizza and say she's going to split it with someone but she'll eat the whole pizza, plus half a loaf of garlic bread. Monica told 'The Insider' "Because of this scandal, I'm a pariah. No man will have me. I'll never get a job wherever I go, whomever I meet, I'm looked at as a freak—the 'other woman.'"

And Ekaete, after she had digested that chunk of misery, felt like Monica. Like the other woman. Having an affair not with Clinton, but with another diet. She was different from the other girls in The Fattening House, this Ekaete.

"That's enough! You've eaten far too much of that *National Enquirer* Ekaete! Girls, I have a surprise for you" exclaimed the old woman making way for some men who tried hard not to look at the girls. They lifted a TV on to a table and informed the room that the satellite dish had been installed.

"I've been watching you Ekaete. Oh yes! And I know what you've been eating from that *National Enquirer*. You want to be Western not so? An American? You want to be thin like them. You equate fat with misery; that's why you're not eating like the rest of the girls."

"Mama!"

"You don't want to be a plump Calabar woman. You don't want people to see we've taken good care of you. And when you marry—because you haven't been putting on weight as you should—who would choose you for a wife? Ekaete you look like a scarecrow. If you marry and don't eat and get fat, people will say your husband isn't taking good care of you!"

She told the girls to sit on the carpeted floor. After they had seen some television show, preferably one that would enforce her opinions on what was getting to be a fatty issue, she would call in some women to help massage the girls' bodies with scented oils; then the girls would have another meal, their last before the day of selection when young men would choose their brides from among the dancing maidens. Maidens, a word, a notion, belonging to the old days when Fattening Houses were Fattening Houses and girls were maidens. Not like Ekaete who refused to eat real food. The old woman had had to succumb to the pleas of some modern thinking people as they called themselves and turn this flat into a Fattening House. And now the satellite dish had been installed, another Western importation provided for the girls so they wouldn't get bored, those people said.

Ekaete again. The girl had had the temerity to switch on the television without asking her permission. Ekaete was sitting close up front staring at the television so that she could see what was going on close up front. "I hope they're not showing any of those film stars like Janet Jackson - she's had ribs removed from her stomach to get thin - and Jane Fonda and Cher. . .they've participated in all sorts of buttocks tucks and. . ."

"Mama" asked one of the girls "How do you know these things?"

"Those film stars are so skinny they look so terrible and they want to please men and at what cost! Now here in Nigeria . . . Oh! Princess Diana! I shall say no more."

Having spoken to Ekaete's mother on the wayward Ekaete the old woman had made it her business to inform herself on the nature of Ekaete's strange diet of American and British magazines prior to the girl's stay in The Fattening House. And she had come to a conclusion. Ekaete was being influenced by Western media. She wanted to be thin because that's what those societies wanted. No matter how much misery those women went through to get thin, stay thin, Ekaete wanted to be fashionably Western and that was why she rejected the Fattening House traditions of her people. Princess Diana's plight would show Ekaete what was what.

But Diana! The old woman gasped—she was so elegant. Paraded in front of their eyes was Diana in designer suits, in evening dresses. So elegant, and so slim. The newscaster said that during her lifetime she was one of the most celebrated and photographed women of all time. She appeared on the covers of *Time* magazine, *Vogue*, *Newsweek*, *Paris Match*. On all the covers. Princess Diana smiled from deep blue eyes, her head a charming tousle of blond hair, her neck curved like a swan's.

The old woman settled herself in an armchair. She chuckled with satisfaction. Most of the girls had been as slim as Princess Diana when they had first entered The Fattening House. But now . . . "Ah!" . . . Involuntarily she clapped her hands, causing some heads to turn. "Sorry girls".

She was sad about Diana's death, but, she reflected, these young girls would see the gruesome effects of dieting...Of wanting to be thin. Ekaete would anyway, and any like minded girl would see the bad things that happen when you slim to please men, instead of following the African way and getting fat and being a credit to your husband. The newscaster was saying that Princess Diana's tragic death in Paris had caused the whole world to mourn. Then followed a procession of glimpses of Diana as a little girl; as a nursery school teacher, the light shining through her dress and showing her legs. Then Princess Diana on the date of her betrothal to Prince Charles of England. In that picture she was fresh, rosy and plump and her hair fell below her eyes as she showed the media, the photographers and newscasters, her engagement ring. The girls in The Fattening House gasped. The ring was a big blue sapphire which matched Princess Diana's eyes. Then in beautiful meandering stream, the fairy-tale wedding of Princess Diana to Prince Charles unfurled . . . the coaches with horses, plumes on their heads and the joyous crowds waving and clapping and cheering. Princess Diana had slimmed, the newscaster said, slimmed especially for her wedding day. Often going for days without food so that she could fit into the wedding dress of ivory lace . . . the flowing long train and the bridesmaids and the flower girls and the page boys and even the groom . . . No one could eclipse the radiant vision, the beauty, the slim figure of the Princess.

Ekaete turned her head to look at the old woman. Turned her head back to the television screen. Left to go to the bathroom. The TV was showing the famous interview which Princess Diana had agreed to, as they say; as she said, "give her side of the story." She spoke of the breach between herself and her husband. And she spoke about her problems with bulimia. It was the first time in their lives that the girls had heard of bulimia. They heard of anorexia and other eating disorders which women develop because of this desperateness to get thin. Princess Diana said she wanted to be thin at any cost. But then hungry she'd raid the fridge and eat. Then she'd go to the bathroom and force herself to vomit the food she had eaten. Then she'd be slim again. Then she'd eat. The girls in The Fattening House were silent. Ekaete came into the room, turned to look at the old woman, her eyes so bitter, so . . .

The old woman shivered and she did not know why. "Change the channel!" she shouted "Change the channel Ekaete!"

Another channel, another station now dwelling on the circumstances surrounding Diana's death.

The old lady switches off the TV. The girls talk. Except

Ekaete.

"Thank goodness, thank goodness our culture is not like that. See, because Diana was forced to be slim, she died."

After the girls have been massaged, plates of food are served and the old woman gives them a talk. It is the last of such talks which she will give to the girls because she knows from experience that they will soon be so sated that they will fall asleep. Even as she speaks some are asleep. She has a cane in her hand and she uses it to tap the television. "Girls! Ekaete are you listening ? Eat up everyone. Ekaete . . .! Poor Princess Diana had all the food she could wish for, and yet because she was a woman in a high position she was forced to have a slim figure and when she ate too much she had to . . ."

"Mama ! We're eating !"

The old woman gives herself a mental pat on the back. Really there is no need to say what she will say but she will say it. The Ekaete types could be dangerous. Could have a bad influence on her girls. Though from the look of her, Ekaete must have digested the dangers of her attitude. She is so silent. The old woman taps the cane on the television. "Here in Nigeria we like our women to be well rounded, our men like us plumpy. Need I say more?"

It was a rhetorical question. Ekaete stood up. "Mama, I think you should know. The man I shall dance for told me he likes me just the way I am. He doesn't care if I'm fat. And he doesn't care if I'm thin. And what's more, I don't care if he cares. Maybe you didn't see me when I got up during the film to go to the bathroom? I had to get rid of Monica Lewinsky, Princess Diana and all the pounded yam and *edi kai ikong*, all the food which you've been trying to stuff down my throat for so many weeks, and, Mama, all of your notions . . . I had to vomit them Mama."

Ekaete didn't wait for a response but stormed out of The Fattening House. And the very next day in all the newspapers and in all the magazines could be seen the very same headline: GIRL STORMS OUT OF FATTENING HOUSE. REFUSES TO EAT ANYTHING-- EVEN THE NIGERIAN NOVEL BY BEN OKRI ENTITLED *THE FAMISHED ROAD*; SAYS SHE WILL FORMULATE HER OWN DIET FROM NOW ON.

When Ekaete saw the headlines she made up her mind to smile a very belly-full smile…and so she did.

The Sokoyokotos

Mr. Sokoyokoto had a dilemma. His wife was so sick that the doctors had told him she had to go to hospital and remain there for three solid months. It wasn't that he didn't care for her; he did, and, moreover, he had the necessary funds to pay her medical bills.

Mr. Sokoyokoto's problem was more profound.

He could only eat meals cooked by his wife. She had always prepared his food exactly to his taste. Indeed, after a culinary-centered courtship, he had married her for the express purpose of having her cook for him, Mr. Sokoyokoto. To date she had concocted the most delicious dishes and snacks ever tasted on the face of this Nigerian earth. Her ewa stews were bean-creamy and the dodo to go with it—why, he often marveled at her expertise in choosing the right plantains and the correct vegetable oil to fry them in. And as for her pounded yam, which she served with *ogbono* soup--it was sheer heaven in his mouth.

Now that she was to go to the hospital and stay there for such a long time, what was he going to do? He asked himself this, his countenance so wracked with consternation that Mrs. Sokoyokoto, who was busy packing her bags in readiness for her trip to the hospital, was moved to comment, "Mr. Sokoyokoto, I won't be gone for too long. And I did cook some stews and deep freeze them. You can warm them up."

Mr. Sokoyokoto was not comforted by this suggestion.

"Mrs. Sokoyokoto," he said, fixing a pair of cold eyes on his woman, "You are my wife. I only eat food prepared by my wife. If I were to follow your advice and warm the stew then I would be the one doing the cooking." He grimaced with pain. "Nevertheless, I suppose we'd better go to the hospital."

The couple drove to the hospital. Mr. Sokoyokoto's face was etched with deep sorrow as he bade goodbye to his wife, Mrs. Sokoyokoto. "I'll visit you tomorrow," he told her. "And I'll come with a big surprise," he concluded, closing the door of the ward. Since in their entire married life, Mr. Sokoyokoto had never brought his wife a surprise, either good or bad, Mrs. Sokoyokoto reflected that perhaps it was opportune that she had to be confined to a hospital bed. Perhaps Mr. Sokoyokoto would appreciate her all the more. Lately she had been feeling that the only reason Mr. Sokoyokoto had married her and turned her into a Mrs. Sokoyokoto was because he wanted a cook for a wife, and for no other reason.

She snuggled into bed and went to sleep, eagerly anticipating Mr. Sokoyokoto's return the next day. And when that day came, she woke up with a start at the commotion around her. Mr. Sokoyokoto had brought several plantains, vegetable oil and beans, and a bag of condiments which he carefully stacked on the bedside table and on the floor. Mrs. Sokoyokoto's eyes grew as big as saucers when she saw her portable kitchen stove. They grew wider when she heard Mr. Sokoyokoto protesting loudly to a group of flabbergasted nurses and a burly looking doctor, "Mrs. Sokoyokoto is my wife! I can't eat anything unless it is cooked by her. Do you people want me to starve? Do you want us both to end up in this hospital?" He tried to shake off their restraining hands and some security men had to be brought in. He was compelled to leave, along with the plantains, vegetable oil, beans, condiments, and the portable stove.

Mrs. Sokoyokoto could not help laughing. Mr. Sokoyokoto had not even greeted her during the fracas. She relaxed in her bed, enjoying her rest.

Mr. Sokoyokoto did not come to the hospital the next day. Mrs. Sokoyokoto thought that it very likely that her husband, Mr. Sokoyokoto, was embarrassed. What with all the fisticuffs and tirades he had been subjected to the previous evening, the man would be too ashamed to come and see her. He did not call her on the telephone either. Well, their telephone was unreliable. Sometimes it worked; often it didn't. That was nothing new; nothing to write home about.

But when he did not come the next day, either, and the days turned into weeks and the weeks turned into the first month since she had left the house, and still, she did not hear from Mr. Sokoyokoto, she became apprehensive; and the doctors and the nurses noticed it. "Is it because your husband hasn't come to see you?" they asked. She nodded.

"Don't worry, Madam. He will soon learn that other people can cook for him—not necessarily his wife. He has no choice," said a nurse. Another held her hand. And somewhat comforted, as she began to recover, Mrs. Sokoyokoto assisted the cooking staff by giving advice from her sickbed—advice that was much appreciated.

Then a nurse brought Mrs. Sokoyokoto a letter. "I believe this is from your husband." The nurse tactfully departed and Mrs. Sokoyokoto ripped the envelope open. She removed the letter. It was type-written and this is how it read:

13 Eshu Street, Lagos

From a suffering husband, Mr. Sokoyokoto, who will suffer no longer.
Date: 13th Feb. forever; millennium

Dear Mrs. Sokoyokoto, the former,

I hope you're having a good time in the hospital, although eating hospital food is not my idea of having a good time.

Because you are going to be away forever, and as I am on the point of starvation, I have married another wife and she is moving in today. This arrangement is best for me. Before you left for the hospital, you insinuated that you would expect your husband, namely me -- at that juncture—to warm stews which you had frozen for me. My heart began to break. I am a man who can only eat meals prepared by his wife. I have not tasted the stews of my new wife but at least she will be my wife and I can begin to eat again.

Try not to take this letter too personally. I have suffered because of your illness. You never warned me that you would fall sick. And when I tried to correct the situation by allowing you to perform your wifely duties by cooking for me in the hospital I was manhandled in the most atrocious inhuman way. Doctors and nurses are supposed to be caring, humane! I had not eaten anything the whole day when I came to see you and I was looking forward to eating food prepared, cooked, freshly cooked by my wife.

During the time you have been away in hospital, apart from my near starvation, my friends have made life unbearable for me. They have jeered when they have seen me eating snacks—mostly groundnuts, which, as you are aware, I am not particularly fond of. Apart from groundnut stew with chicken, the groundnuts to the best of my knowledge cannot really be cooked by wives. When my friends see me buying groundnuts, they find me ridiculous, or pitiable. On that diet I felt as if I was very low in their eyes, ground level. In fact I was going nuts.

I am not sure — at this juncture – that I shall be able to pay your medical bills because of the hefty dowry I had to pay for the new Mrs. Sokoyokoto. From now on, use your maiden name, because the new Mrs. Sokoyokoto will come to my house this evening.

I must sign off now because the new Mrs. Sokoyokoto is coming. She plans to cook *ewa* and *dodo*. Don't try to contact me. My mind is made up.

Yours, your former husband

Mr. Sokoyokoto

Mrs. Sokoyokoto the former showed the letter to the doctors and nurses, who immediately agreed that as soon as she felt well enough she would be employed full time as chief cook in the hospital. She would be given accommodation and a fat salary. She would not be called Mrs. Sokoyokoto but would devise a new name for herself, whatever name she would like.

Utterly comforted, and drifting off into sleep, the former Mrs. Sokoyokoto heard the ring-ring of the telephone at her bedside table. The phone was working after all and Mr. Sokoyokoto was asking, "Did you receive my letter?"

She said she had received it, and he went on, "I had to tell someone about what I've been going through, and you are the only one I know to call. Now I have found that the new Mrs. Sokoyokoto's *ewa* and *dodo* are uneatable. I don't suppose you would care to come back home? I think I'm prepared to wait it

56

out."

Mrs. Sokoyokoto that was, told him no, she was not returning home.

"In that case," said Mr. Sokoyokoto resignedly, "I must marry yet another wife to cook my meals. I just don't know what's happening in this Nigeria. And you know what? You were never a genuine Mrs. Sokoyokoto. No wife of mine, no real Mrs. Sokoyokoto would have told me to warm up frozen stews. I don't care if I eat groundnuts for days on end, I'm going to make sure that when I marry again it will be to a real Mrs. Sokoyokoto."

After this wonderful news, Mrs. Sokoyokoto got out of bed in a surge of health and well being; dressed, and left her ward. The doctors, the nurses, the patients, and the visitors saw a woman with purpose in her gait and in her whole mien striding toward the kitchen. Those who knew her situation were not surprised at her complete and sudden recovery.

In Tact

Olokun, the Goddess of the Ocean, gazed into the mirror before her and turned her head lazily. Yes, the necklace definitely did set off her ocean beauty. Smiling, she touched the necklace with its sapphires, pearls and crystal droplets of insouciance strung on silver threads which glimmered and glimmered about her neck. It did indeed set off her beauty to perfection, and when the visitors from the astral world saw her they would be so overpowered--so impressed---even that wretched so and so *Orunmila*, the Chief God of all the gods, couldn't measure up to the necklace. He might be, chief God, but she was the Goddess of the Ocean, *Olokun*. She whispered her name, "*Olokun*." And the name rivered round her in mellifluous melodies as she shook her long water-falling hair.

The throne room had been decorated to her satisfaction. The goldfish, the whales and the octopuses were in their places. The mermen and the mermaids had even seduced a special rainbow from the sky, and the rainbow had agreed to hang on the wall behind her agate- studded throne.

Again she touched her necklace. She had had it for years. On a special occasion much like that envisaged for this very morning, that—that deplorable Chief God *Orunmila* had lent her the necklace. She had promised to return it on the very day she borrowed it but the days had grown into months, the months into years and gradually somehow the necklace

58

became hers. Now it completely belonged to her, the Goddess of the Ocean, *Olokun*. She was glad she had held onto it. What other piece of jewellery would so powerfully impress the astral world elite?

"No other," she gurgled gleefully. And with a majestic sashay, she sailed-swished down the underwater hallway, its walls embedded with precious sea stones. In the throne room, her guests were already there, waiting. Waiting for her, the Goddess of the Ocean, *Olokun*.

****

Meanwhile in the earthly realm, the president of Nigeria, Mr. Fagbemi, was eating breakfast with his First Wife, Mrs. Fagbemi Number One.

"I can't take it any longer," said Mrs. Fagbemi.

"What can't you take?" asked Mr. Fagbemi, folding his newspaper.

His wife bit into a slice of toast with melancholic savagery.

"What? Mr. Fagbemi, you know very well what I can't take!"

"It certainly isn't toast."

"Mr. Fagbemi, you are president of this great nation, Nigeria. Correct me if I'm wrong."

"You are right, Mrs. Fagbemi, Number-One wife. You are right. I am the president of this great nation Nigeria. What of it?"

"And we are having a dinner party tonight, are we not?"

"Right again, Mrs. Fagbemi. Just a small affair. I want you and my second wife to arrange the cooking. By the way, have you decided on the entrée? Is it to be fish or crab?"

"There will be no dinner party tonight unless I get my

necklace back from the Minister's wife."

"Not that again. Why don't you let it rest? You should have known that when you lent her the necklace you wouldn't be able to ask for it again. Why, it has been years . . ."

"I want to wear my necklace at the dinner party tonight."

"You should concentrate on the menu, Mrs. Fagbemi Number-One wife. Have you and your junior wife decided on fish or crab? I need to know before I go to the office. I want to personally order them."

"You, a whole President! Ordering fish or crab!"

"Yes, Mrs. Fagbemi, number- one."

"I want my necklace. I want my necklace from the Minister's wife!"

"No. Mrs. Fagbemi Number-One."

Mrs. Fagbemi was upset. Mr. Fagbemi folded his newspaper and slipped it into the briefcase at his side. "If you're so anxious to retrieve your necklace -- and really I can't think why after all these years -- just go and get it."

Mrs. Fagbemi's eyebrows rose.

"Get dressed, Mrs. Fagbemi, and I'll take you in my car, how's that? Then after you've seen the Minister's wife, phone me and let me know what you've decided for the menu tonight."

"Fish or crab!" cried Mrs. Fagbemi gleefully, and hurried away to dress for her visit. When she returned to Mr. Fagbemi, who was waiting patiently, he was somewhat surprised at the sequined *buba* and wrapper she wore. Oh how they glittered and glittered!

****

The goddess *Olokun*, ocean-smiling, bathed in waves of adulation as her astral world visitors gushed; their mouths oohing and ah-ing, their eyes directed at her necklace in a most gratifying way. And--but was she imagining it ? No; it couldn't be; but it was--Fish, First Wife of Chief God *Orunmila*!

Fish had sauntered into her presence. Fish, with her fishy smell and her revolting sequined scaly gown and her rimless eyes. How had she managed to get past the mermen guards and the octopuses with their heavily ammunitioned arms?

Chief God *Orunmila* must have sent Fish. There stood the visitors from the astral world before her-- and Fish was in their midst. In their midst was—the Goddess *Olokun* could feel it-- embarrassment.

Revolting Fish! Her voice was a lisping soprano lilt which was so high pitched that it caused *Olokun*'s neck to ache; her very necklace to tremble in vibrating chords. And these chords at that moment, unannounced, decided to enter her throat and erupt from her mouth into "Why have you come here, Fish?"

Fish was a big fish. She smoothed her sequined gown over her rounded belly.

"*Olokun*, I'm so sorry to have interrupted this, this--" she appraised the astral visitors—"this gathering. But I'll get straight to the point. Your Chief God, *Orunmila*, wants his necklace back. He lent you the necklace years ago and you haven't bothered to return it."

Fish squinted at the necklace. "Hmm *Olokun*, I see you've added some new stones to the necklace. Kindly remove them and I'll . . ."

Olokun forced a wave from her majestic curve of body and in a hot water voice shouted at some eager octopuses, whose tentacles were at the ready, to tentacle Fish.

"And when you've tentacled her in, whip her well!" she ordered.

61

How dare Fish? How had she dared to enter the throne room? And as for demanding the necklace! *Olokun* gasped for breath. Within seconds she was surrounded by mermaids who did their best to revive her water spirits with watered spirits. Fish was tentacled and then she was tentacled some more. And in spite of their instructions to whip Fish quite well, the octopuses flogged Fish quite badly. In fact she was so badly beaten that her arms and her legs dropped off and she had to swim back to Chief God *Orunmila* using stumps which today are called fins by those in the know. She had to slither her way, armless and legless, up the stairs into the palace living room where Chief God *Orunmila* awaited her.

****

Mr. Fagbemi, true to his word, took Mrs. Fagbemi Number One to the mansion of the Minister and then drove off to his office. What with the dinner party, and with the entrée fish or crab still undecided, it was going to be a long day.

It would be even more of a long day for Mrs. Fagbemi Number One.

She was escorted into one of the many plush rooms of the mansion and what she saw made her choke with indignation. The Minister's wife was wearing that necklace. Her own necklace. The necklace of Mrs. Fagbemi Number One. And what was more, the wives of the ambassadors of the oceans of the world-- the Atlantic, the Indian, the Pacific and the Arctic and most likely the Antartic oceans—were winding round and round the room volubly admiring the necklace around the neck of the Minister's wife.

Then Mrs. Fagbemi spoke, "I'll be brief Minister's wife. I'm having a dinner party tonight--you're invited of course--and I want my necklace back."

And in the horrified silence which gulped the news, she added, "and I want it now!"

The Minister's wife issued tight-lipped directives to some butlers in the vicinity and a frustrated, angry Mrs. Fagbemi found herself propelled outside the ministerial mansion with bruises on her arms and with the sequins torn off her dress. But she did have her mobile phone in her hand and she called her husband.

"Mr. Fagbemi, oh, Mr. Fagbemi, my sequins have fallen off —"

"Did you get the necklace, Mrs. Fagbemi, Number-One wife?"

"No. Mr. Fagbemi, I--"

"Are we having fish or crab tonight?" was the only other question Mr. Fagbemi asked Mrs. Fagbemi, his Number-One wife.

****

The Chief God, *Orunmila* nodded with his crown on his head, which was not as simple an action as one might suppose because the crown was very heavy. His First Wife, Fish, had just related her experience with goddess *Olokun*. *Orunmila* told Fish to relax in a special aquarium which he had constructed for a fish with such injuries as these. Then he ordered one of his assistants to fetch his Second Wife, Crab Akon.

The crab waddled her way to the *Orunmila* throne, and with her eyes literally bulging out on tentacles, stood to crab-tention.

"Sir, My Chief God, *Orunmila*, I've just seen Fish. This is awful! How could your messenger have been subjected to such treatment! It's awful!"

"I'm glad you used that word, Crab Akon"

"Sir?"

"Awful. The situation is not only awful. It is also filled with awe."

Orunmila gave Crab Akon some time to absorb the implications of that particular sentiment and then instructed her on the gentle art of persuasion. Surely if she used the utmost diplomacy, she could retrieve a borrowed necklace, even from no less a personage than the Goddess of the Ocean, *Olokun*.

And with the instructions of *Orunmila* guiding her on her way, Crab Akon waddled to the ocean home of *Olokun*.

The octopuses, the mermen, the mermaids and the great Goddess of the Ocean herself, *Olokun*, were there.

Olokun seemed to have recovered from the episode with Fish and she was richly confluenting smooth as the astral dignitaries continued to bow and pay her homage with a most delicious obeisance. They had brought her gifts of moons, suns, planets and thousands of stars which sparkled in heaps around her throne.

As she approached *Olokun*, Mrs. Crab Akon rocked to this side and to that. She whispered into the shell ears of *Olokun* who with a flowing majesty, rivered out of the palace room and into an adjoining apartment, with the crab following. *Olokun* told her attendants to leave her alone with Mrs. Crab Akon. The octopuses sulked. You could see sulk written all over their tentacles. But they had been ordered to leave Mrs. Crab Akon and Goddess *Olokun* alone; so they did.

Mrs. Crab Akon first praised the great might and beauty of the goddess. She even said that she was so beautiful that she had no need of any ornament. She herself was an ornament. This was a tricky moment. *Olokun* asked Mrs. Crab Akon if she was an ornament and only an ornament. But Mrs. Crab Akon gently dismissed these remarks.

With such visitors from the astral world coming to see her, such gifts, such homage, the Goddess's beauty was transparently clear even without the necklace.

Then came the moment—and it was a moment of great moment—to ask for the necklace. Mrs. Crab Akon said tentacal-tively, "I have come, dear one, to collect the thing from you." Then she said the sentence in Yoruba to give the Goddess *Olokun* sufficient time to remove from around her neck the necklace in question which was no longer in question: *Orun umila ni ki in gbe kim yem wa?*

When she left the court with the necklace, Crab fairly skidded over the sands so anxious was she to reach the palace of *Orunmila*.

Without a word, *Orunmila* placed the necklace around his own neck and went to the aquarium to see Fish. The fish looked up at him with fish eyes.

"You've got the necklace, I see, sir."

"Yes, Fish, I have indeed. It is a shame about your arms and legs—not having them I mean—but you'll be able to swim better in the sea, won't you, Fish?"

"Which sea, sir? Which ocean, sir?"

"Why, Fish, any sea and any ocean," said *Orunmila*, fingering his necklace.

"Does this mean I've been demoted, sir?" inquired Fish, her gills flapping.

"Not at all. As a matter of fact I'm appointing you Head of Schools of Fish. You may be able to teach others a thing or two from your experience."

So Fish jumped out of the aquarium to begin her new assignment. She decided that for her offices, she would leave oceans well alone. She would conduct her teaching assignments in rivers before the rivers ran into oceans.

****

Mr. Fagbemi picked up his telephone to call his second wife. "Mrs. Fagbemi, Number Two?"

And he advised her on the most diplomatic way to retrieve the necklace from the Minister's wife. Mrs.Fagbemi Number Two howled. How could she succeed where Wife Number One had failed she asked him with rising consternation. The consternation rose so much that it zoomed through the telephone and it hit Mr. Fagbemi causing his head to reel. He and his wives—Mrs. Fagbemi Number One and Mrs. Fagbemi Number Two--had yet to decide on whether they would have fish or crab for their dinner party.

Mrs. Fagbemi Number Two soon found herself at the mansion of the Minister's wife. The Minister's wife was still there and so were the wives of the ambassadors, and so were the butlers and so was the necklace.

Parting her way through the company Mrs. Fagbemi Number Two whispered into the ears of the Minister's wife and the women disappeared into an adjoining room. Mrs. Fagbemi Number Two praised the Minister's wife. The latter always attracted so many dignitaries to her household. She was a symbol of what the nation, the very country, stood for.

"And what is that?" asked the Minister's wife.

"Everything," replied Mrs. Fagbemi Number Two. This was a tricky moment.

"Everything?" repeated the minister's wife.

Mrs. Fagbemi Number Two told her that she stood for everything that was good and upright and the Minister's wife relaxed and promptly sat down. She began to remove the necklace even before Mrs. Fagbemi Number Two asked for it and the two women embraced.

****

Mr. Fagbemi was on the telephone again. His first wife sat on a chair tugging at a shawl draped around her shoulders.

"It's fine. My second wife has your necklace," he told her lowered head. "Everything's in tact now," he said, "And, my dear, we must make a decision about the entrée for tonight!"

He looked at his wife.

"Is the air conditioner too much for you? Why are you wearing a shawl?"

Mrs. Fagbemi exposed her badly bruised arms.

"I see, I see" the president murmured, and then in a bantering way he added *Eja in bakan*? Is your decision fish or crab my dear?"

Mrs. Fagbemi asked tearfully, "So my junior wife got the necklace and I did not?"

"No, my dear, you did not. And my advice to you is to get rid of that tattered, sequined outfit."

Mrs. Fagbemi Number One complied. And that night crab was served as the entrée at their dinner party. Mrs. Fagbemi Number Two, feeling quite joyous at her victory in obtaining the necklace, tactfully co-operated with her husband's wishes and agreed to also serve fish---on the side.

The Bone Eater

He came with his teeth, clad in expensive *asoke* and armed with his teeth which, with the aid of his jaws, opened and shut, shut and opened so that they appeared like an ancient portcullis shutting and opening as he sat down in the best armchair in the living room, an insolent sprawl in his hips, a dribble of sympathy for the deceased rimmed round his mouth of teeth.

"You must be the daughter, the sister, the aunt, the grandmother, the daughter-in-law of poor Mrs. Durojaiye?"

Mrs. Durojaiye was my Aunt Lola and she had died and the funeral was over.

It had lasted for days and the guests, friends and relatives had finally left after eating many sumptuous funeral feasts in celebration of her death. Aunt Lola had died at the ripe old age of ninety-five and during her life she had been a prominent, wealthy lady. Lots of people came from Lagos, Kaduna, Owerri all the way to Ibadan where our family house rested on tall pillars above green lawns for the funeral. But now that was all over and I was alone in the house until this man came into our living room, unannounced, with his teeth.

He says he knows the entire family of Durojaiye except me. I'm the only one he doesn't know. From my accent I must be a *Tokunbo* relative who spent some time abroad or else he would have recognized me as a Durojaiye. Didn't I see him at the funeral? The funeral feast was wonderful. He had come to pay his respects to the bereaved. And where were the other family members?

I didn't explain that my family, tired from supervising the cooking for the funeral and serving to hundreds of people, had long since gone to their respective homes. I didn't mind, especially because the funeral, the feast, had been such a success.

Everything had gone well and everyone had eaten as much as they could and more. Except this man, apparently. He asked me for a plate of fried chicken—something of a specialty at the funeral. I obliged.

"This is delicious!" he cried "Pure Agric Nigerian chicken!"

Chomping with rapid ease, he told me that he had spent a number of years in England and had eaten the frozen chicken which that country sold in its many supermarkets. Alone, without his family and cold, he had not enjoyed that chicken.

"Ah! But this is true Nigerian chicken. This is the best chicken I've eaten, ever eaten at any funeral . . . And I can tell you I attend many, many funerals. Oh yes! This is true Agric!"

The chicken, he said, flashing his teeth, was tough and strong and he could really get his incisors into it.

"Incisors?"

"Incisors, my eye teeth— and my molars, come to think of it. When I can," he declared, smacking his lips, "I buy my chicken live from the market. No frozen chicken for me. It makes me lonely and cold."

I had, of course, seen the chickens he spoke of; they were usually cooped up in baskets in the markets and most people preferred to buy them live and then personally kill them before eating. The chickens supposedly had a better, more authentic flavour than their frozen English counterparts—bought from supermarkets. He was expatiating.

"I take the chicken to my yard and I cut its neck so!"

He left off eating to form his fingers in the shape of a knife, leapt from his chair, and laughingly repeated "So!" and he pushed his fingers; jabbed them at my neck.

I did not say anything, and he returned to his chair.

"Delicious and well seasoned," he said, and was suddenly dejected, for the chicken meal was now at an end. "I'm sorry Mrs. Durojaiye died."

He perused the room with his incisors.

"It's good that she has rich children and grandchildren to give her such a grand send-off! And what delicious chicken! Real Nigerian Agric!"

I had thought that he would now leave. He had, after all, eaten. But he settled himself in my chair.

"Do you people have any video films? It's been a while since I've watched a good film. If I had thought of it before I would have suggested that you serve me the Agric chicken along with a film!"

"I'm afraid that's the last of the chicken. It was good of you to come. Thanks so much."

"What about the film? You look like a family that would have access to good films."

He rose and walked to a table on which were perched three films, video cassettes. He read the blurb on the back of one of them, appropriately titled 'Chocolat,' and extracting the cassette from its cover, popped it into the video machine.

"Which one is the video channel?" he enquired, while methodically pressing the control until the film came into view.

"I'm really tired," I began, "what with the cooking, the

whole funeral—"

"No problem! Why don't you go to bed? Your brothers and sisters have gone home. You need some rest. I can see that. Are you sure there's no more Agric chicken? Or any other type? I don't really mind."

"Of course you don't," I whispered savagely.

Fearing that if I did do that—carry out his suggestion and go to sleep—he would tour the house and eat the supplies for the week, I decided to sit out the film with him; tired as I was.

But I couldn't keep my eyes open and I dreamed a dream. In the dream this Agric chicken eater, had rampaged the cupboards in the kitchen; the freezer had been emptied of its contents and the atmosphere was a veritable machination of chompings, munchings, gulpings and lip smackings. But this itself did not disturb me.

In my dream, the man, having demolished every item of food in the house, began on the house proper. I saw him concocting a meal. A three-course affair. For the appetizer he ate the windows and doors made up in a kind of window-door melee. For his main course he ate the walls and the floors. Huge slabs, stuffing living room walls; the walls of the bedroom, the kitchen walls, down his mouth; in wall after wall after wall. For desert he ate everything that was left.

I screamed in my sleep, and, opening my eyes I had a good glimpse of his teeth. They were teeth of the grave yard in a funeral mouth of dark and they stood out sharply. Huge, white, mortared, chiselled. Like the slabs which covered my dead aunt Lola.

"The film was great! Chocolat!" he enthused, "You must have been having a nightmare!"

We were now in the wee hours of the morning.

"Are there any ailments in the Durojaiye family? Any inherent diseases? Is there anyone alive who is still . . . Mrs. Durojaiye took a long time to die didn't she ?"

I ground my own teeth and he left without saying goodbye. I was sure he'd be back.

And he was; dressed very expensively again, in another *agbada* of *asoke*. He said that he had heard that the Durojaiye family were about to distribute food to the neighbours as was the custom.

"We have a fantastic tradition here in Yoruba land!" he exclaimed, his teeth flashing.

There hadn't been time to clean up the room the night before so I proceeded to stack the dirty dishes preparatory to having them washed. It dawned on me . . . like that . . . there was nothing to clean. There was nothing to throw away. There were no chicken bones to be seen. He was the only one around during the gap of time between the end of the funeral and this very morning . . . and . . .

"Did you eat everything? The bones?"

He shrugged his shoulders.

"I'm asking you . . . did you eat the chicken bones last night?"

"Chicken bones are very nutritious. They have bone marrow. Very healthy."

"You ate not only your chicken bones, but the bones of others, other guests, as well?"

"Why yes. Is that a crime? Doesn't it save you from having to throw them away?"

He lazed around the whole day, but made sure to follow the servers to our neighbours and he ate and he ate. He returned at nightfall with a request to see yet another film, perhaps 'Soul Food'.

"Sorry I'm going to sleep."

He didn't appear to have heard so I left him in disgust and retired to my bedroom.

This time I had a dreamless sleep. When I awoke it was almost mid-day and trying to slip from my bed I found my legs dangling in space. Crawling on bits of floor, I went, my eyes still sleepy, to the bathroom to wash my face. There was no sink. I could not see the walls dividing room from room either. Was I dreaming? Was I just plain tired? In the areas which used to be rooms I saw just more spaces covered by a hot malignant sun. Only the cold floor alerted me to the knowledge that this was in no way a dream. As I stood resting on a pillar—yes the pillars of the house remained—I saw in the distance my neighbours, a crowd of them, pointing.

Screams were rising into the sky and a noise overpowered those screams. A chiselling-chip-by-chip-chiselling.

Hopping from one piece of floor to another, I noticed that my furniture had vanished.

There were no windows and doors either. Nothing. Only this vacuumed vacancy of space in which I ran. That chiselling chip-by-chip noise was coming from him of course . . .The Bone Eater. His teeth worked up and down in an energy of movement; deliberate; devouring; sharply-concise.

"You didn't leave me any chicken, not even a single chicken bone to munch on!" he whined.

"Are you saying that you ate my house, my furniture, my windows, all because I didn't leave you chicken or chicken bones?"

"Well, you didn't, did you?" he asked with confident indignation.

"You snacked on my house? This is unbelievable!"

I couldn't even get dressed, because naturally he had eaten my clothes too.

"I'm sorry I ate most of your house. Honestly I am...but..."

"You're sorry you ate my house?"

"Well I didn't eat everything!"

"You, you Bone Eater!" was the only expletive I could manage.

"First I thought I'd have a snack" he said, "And then . . . those video films are very good . . . and then I got really hungry and I just ate and ate."

"I must be the first woman in the history of this Nigerian world to have her house eaten by a Bone Eater"

"No you're not," he said wagging his head, "As a matter of fact, this is my business. I am the Chief executive of Bone Eater Incorporated."

"Pardon?"

"I, we, go around to people's houses in Nigeria—my area is Akure, that's my bone eating beat as it were—and we eat. Whenever there is a wedding feast, a birthday party and of course, funerals, we're there. From experience I've discovered that funerals are the best. We of Bone Eater Incorporated thrive on funeral feasts. It's our way of expressing a feeling of community. I used to be so alone in England with that cold chicken. And Madam, "he paused, "we usually consume the pillars of the houses too."

"Why didn't you eat mine? You've eaten everything else. Don't bother to answer. I slept for too long. Had I slept any longer you might have eaten me too—including my bones!"

His eye teeth were coated by sobriety when he said, "Madam, we of Bone Eater Incorporated, I, myself, would

74

never eat the likes of you, Madam."

He was perusing a pillar of my house. Or what was left of it.

"Madam," he pronounced, "your responsibility as a member of the elite is to ensure that you have very old, very wealthy relatives like Mrs. Durojaiye on the point of death and you and them must build more houses. Buy them if you like . . . It's your debt to society Madam. You must build houses, host lots of funerals where Agric chicken is served and so on. You must not neglect your . . ."

I wasn't listening. The dream, this Bone Eater, the funeral, the eating of my house, my furniture and my clothing had made me downright ravenous. I too have very sharp incisors; and . . . I was suddenly very hungry . . .

And expensive *asoke*-clad men, bones and all . . . expensive *asoke* clad men don't taste that bad.

The Difference Is Clear

"If I were you sir . . ." broached the Minister's wife as she helped her husband drape a gold cord around his uniformed chest; as she flicked an imaginary speck of dust from the Minister's broad front resplendent with shiny jagged edged metals which nearly scratched her hesitant fingers, "If I were you sir . . ."

"Well, you're not me, are you ?" boomed the Minister, the sound causing the mantelpiece to shake and the long mirror in front of which he stood to wobble. "You're not me. You are not the Minister of an important no-nonsense government like ours, so shut up."

The couple looked at their reflections. The Minister was so tall that he had to duck his head so that he could see his head, and this despite the fact that he had had the longest mirror ordered from New York to accommodate his stature. He regarded the bushy eyebrows with satisfaction, the clean shaven protrusion of the angular jaw, the elongated eyes which darted up and down and he sighed, lifted his head and perused the rest of his form spruce as it was; natty; decked out in military uniform.

His wife, broadly squat, with anxious jabbering movements, hovered behind him. The Minister whirled around smartly.

"Wife I am going to this election to cast my vote and that's that. I'm tired of foreign nations trying to dictate to Nigeria what and what we should not do. Do we do that to them? No we do not. Democracy should be seen clearly for what it is. Nigerian democracy is a specialized democracy."

He stepped back from the mirror and turned to appraise himself from a side view. He was headless of course, but he looked smart. His entire uniform from every angle revealed a confident no-nonsense Minister of the higher echelons of a no-nonsense government. His medals shone as did his shoes, which his wife had polished days before in readiness for Election Day.

"I'm the one in the government whose been doing all the campaigning. There won't be any trouble so you can keep your opinions to yourself."

"Sir" ventured his wife, her arms hanging limply before her. "I, I, don't understand. I thought you were only, um, I mean . . ."

"That's what I mean by you being a wife and me being a Minister."

"The difference is clear sir, Minister sir."

"Not making a joke at my expense are you?"

The Minister was referring to an advertisement which posited the joys of drinking a soft drink called "7UP". A stick man frolicked and cavorted across the screens of televisions throughout the length and breadth of Nigeria and drank a colourless liquid—the 7 UP in question—through a straw, and then after much gurgling and slurping noises in which the green bottle of 7UP distinction appeared, a deep baritone voice was heard to say "7UP. The difference is clear." The drink and the slogan which accompanied it had become so popular that the government had decided to use it in their political campaigns.

With a difference! The Minister himself had toured the country with several representatives of the 7UP bottling company to the chagrin of other soft drink companies like Coca Cola and Fanta who did not have the obvious advantage of being colourless---Coca Cola being darky-browny and Fanta bright orange—and the Minister had when he mounted the various podiums, drunk a bottle of 7 U P with a straw, his bushy eyebrows drawn together in serious concentration and then to an intrigued crowd declaring "In the coming elections you people must vote for us. We are a strict government. We do not allow any hanky panky. That is why we have prevented any competing parties from participating in the forthcoming elections. Besides . . ."

And here the Minister would pause for effect, drink rapidly from another bottle of 7UP with another straw and declare in much the same way as the advertisements did "The difference is clear."

It was an intriguing and even persuasive argument. Intriguing because to the crowds who listened in the often hot-blinding sun, since there was no different party by which to ascertain the difference between the government's party and the other parties which were non-existent, it wasn't apparently clear why there was a difference and why, even if the difference could be clearly imagined why that difference would be clear. What was, however, clear to the crowd listening in the hot sun were the free drinks supplied by 7UP and the Minister and the Minister's government.

The crowds would cheer, toss their caps and *geles* and handkerchiefs up into the sky and promise the government victory. They were happy that the opposition parties had been more or less banned. And they loved 7UP.

"You can't stop me from clearly casting my vote Wife. And that's that."

The woman seemed to shrivel.

"I wasn't going to ask you not to go," she murmured, "I just want you to be careful my Minister husband."

The Minister towered above her, his words like the bullets he carried, along with his neat silver gun snug under his jacket.

"Let's be clear about this. Let's be very clear. The people love me in the same way they love 7UP—if not more."

The Minister's eyebrows collapsed into a straight bushy line.

"The difference is clear. What's more . . ." he drawled, "We're going to be elected. This government is going to be in power yet again for some fifty years or so. I've seen the crowds slurping down their 7UP. They like it and they like us."

****

The Minister had some time left before he went to cast his vote. It was a mere exercise and the thought brought a smile to his lips and he decided to indulge his wife as to the underlying philosophy of his political 7UP strategy. He would allow his wife this explanation, and most fortuitously the time scheduled for his departure from the house was exactly the amount of minutes it took for a 7UP commercial to be broadcast on the television. The stick man danced before his eyes as he sketched out for his wife his 7UP campaign philosophy.

The bottle in which the 7UP lived was green and the 7 and the UP was written on it in white. Green and white were Nigeria's nationalistic colours. It was a nationalistic drink with nationalistic colours on the outside of the bottle.

Then there was the 7 on the bottle; a very special number, especially for the Christian population. It took God seven days to create the world and the governing government had been in power for seven years. This was no coincidence and it was very clear.

The UP of 7 UP meant, or signified that when the government was elected for another seven years then of course they were on their way UP—not that they had ever been down of course—

Lastly, there was a dense red circle on the bottle, and since red was an exciting colour and a circle was a circle, signifying the never-ending circular reign of the ruling government, then it followed that Nigeria and its peoples were in for an exciting round red circular time of governmental continuity.

The Minister rose to his full length, walked to the mirror, crouched to see his head, then extended his neck and saw his headless body again before quitting his mansion for the polling booth. His limousine which sported a whining siren and a dense red circle of a light-globe on its bonnet cover whirred as he sped through the streets of Victoria Island. In front of his car were two others with blackened windows which screamed his ministerial presence, and the limousine was flanked by several outriders on motor cycles. Army jeeps took up the rear filled with soldiers dressed in their military gear. They had whips in their hands with which to beat anyone who got in their way. And behind them several hefty trailers lumbered, their confines loaded with crates of 7UP. The Minister planned to have them distributed to the voters at the polling booth, and since the day promised to be hot with parched skies filled with empty-bellied clouds, he was sure the 7UP would be consumed rapidly.

"What's up? What in the 7 is up?" he shouted.

He could not, dared not believe his eyes. It was worse when he was helped out of his car and heard what he heard; and then he couldn't believe the sight of his ears. There, right next to the polling booth was one of the would-be contestants who had been prevented from forming a party; why, the man and the other party opposition leaders had had several dinners at his house and had been given enough 7UP to last them a life time. To a man they had agreed NOT to run against the government's electioneering campaigns. And now . . . now on Election Day . . .

"Bring me my mobile phone," shouted the Minister.

His worst fears were confirmed. Throughout the nation, at every polling booth, the formerly silent opposition party leaders were exhorting, encouraging the people to vote for them; one of them and NOT the government. And, irony of ironies, they were employing the very same identical slogan as he had--

7UP THE DIFFERENCE IS CLEAR

--to rally the crowd to their side. Sitting in his limousine he tuned the car radio to Oyo, Abuja, Rivers State, Anambra . . . the leaders of the opposition parties—so they had dared to be oppositional! And they were saying the same thing! It was a concerted movement against the government. His jaw dropped, his bushy eyebrows clambered down to the region just above the bridge of his nose; and the gold cord looped on his jacket slumped; and his medals became moist and his shiny shoes lost their shine as he heard –

"And these are the reasons why each and every Nigerian of eligible age should vote for any one of the opposition parties and NOT for the existing government—the difference is clear. The green and white colours on the 7UP bottle represent democracy which has been wilted of late—in the new bottles—it was true it was a brighter green—the green represents new growth and the white, purity—it was also a new white and the Minister hissed with regret at not having polished his own 7UP bottles.

The voice continued ruthlessly:

The 7 is a number of creation but the 7 has to be created by us, by you, by God. The 7 on the government's bottle means that it's a stagnant lean 7 year government; we have to have a vibrant 7. It is only then we can go up.

As for the red spot—the Minister cringed involuntarily—if we, if Nigeria continues in this way, the red will speak blood.

It will be a blemish on our nation. Let us make the red in us a new revolutionary red. Furthermore, although the difference is 7 Uply clear, we as Nigerians must add some colour to our lives, and that is why we welcome not only 7UP activists in our midst but Coco-colites, Fantites and every other soft drink affiliate, activist, to form a new government.

The crowds listened, heard, saw that the difference which they always knew anyway—in a thirsty-I'll-drink-you-for-now-way-but-I'll-wait-for-the-right-time-drinking-way-----that they would cast their vote for one of the opposition parties. The difference had always been clear; even when they were thirsty, the difference had always been uply clear.

Manufactured *Pon Mon*

"It's getting to be a bit of a problem," declared Alhaji Mustafa.

"Yes sah, Minister sah," cried his host, a wealthy business tycoon, who had invited the honourable Minister Alhaji Mustafa to a sumptuous dinner. And the guests were sumptuously clad as was the anticipated dinner. Velvet *agbadas* flowed in rich mauves and reds; guinea brocade of gold and silver also flowed sumptuously.

But the host felt un-sumptuous. He did not quite follow the argument of the Minister, and it was necessary at least to pretend that he did. Having made his millions through nefarious means, he had played the honesty-not-so-honesty tricks to the hilt. It was a strange kind of honesty but it had served him well. His favourite words were, "I'm a plain and down to earth man. A son of the soil." He pronounced son as "shon" and soil as "shoil" indicating to all and sundry that he was indeed a son of the soil.

He was dressed in simple down to earth peasant garb, even now, at this dinner to which he had invited those who were not really true sons of the soil like him. They had intellect, a superior wisdom, he told them. It was because of their intellect, their advice, that he was now the millionaire he was. He had invited them to an honest dinner where they were told in advance that he would serve only Nigerian upper class food.

Everything on the menu had *a la* attached to it. There was *a la* pepper soup; *a la ogbono* and *a la* pounded yam. Maybe after the dinner they would change, especially the Minister of Engineering, Alhaji Mustafa, would change his mind about the future of the *Pon Mon* business in Nigeria. The business which depends on *Pon Mon*.

But the many *a las* which the guests perceived, were accompanied by titters from the ladies and guffaws from the men.

And none of those titters and guffaws were *a la* like anything he had ever encountered before. He was feeling distinctly un*alahed.* They didn't appreciate him. He was poor in taste. He was a shon of the shoil. He hadn't even had the courage to give them his favourite dish of *Pon Mon*. True he had an *a la* attached to it; but somehow when the honourable Minister had declared in intellectual tones that *Pon Mon* was getting to be a bit of a problem and he couldn't quite fathom the argument, his cheeks tightened. He felt ashamed. Downright ashamed.

The Minister cut his meat in the *ogbono* stew and when the slimy mixture drew the host felt slimy. Unaccountably so.

The Minister was saying that food and class were synonymous.

Certain classes of people ate certain classes of food. *Pon Mon* was low class food. Nigerians should not eat *Pon Mon* anymore. He was determined to re-orient this state of affairs during his tenure as the newly appointed Minister of Engineering, "*Pon Mon* is nothing but cow-hide, cow-skin" said Alhaji Mustafa, "and people are enjoying, actually enjoying *Pon Mon*. It's a disgrace. We have to do something about our tastes. Apart from that, Nigeria's leather industry is suffering because people are literally eating prospective handbags and shoes."

"Ah!" exclaimed the host, "You don't mean it! I did think say that they done eat the skin *pata pata*. I no say they eat manufactured *Pon Mon*. But then, I am only shon of the shoil."

"Of course they don't eat shoes and handbags, but they are literally eating into our leather trade. What we need is a change of attitude."

"Latitude sah?"

"Attitude. Attitude."

Thinking of his *Pon Mon* stew in the kitchen the host coughed to hide his embarrassment. But oh, how he loved *Pon Mon*. You could chew it and keep it in your mouth for a long time. His *Pon Mon* business was thriving and now the powers that be wanted Nigerians to desist from eating *Pon Mon*. The dinner could not come to an end too quickly for the host. What would happen to the millions of Nigerians who loved *Pon Mon* as he did?

"I expected you as a *Pon Mon* magnate to have just a little Pon Mon at this dinner, my host. The very reason for this dinner is for you to persuade us why *Pon Mon* should not be discontinued for the good of the nation, the Nigerian people."

"Sah ?"

"A man with your business acumen . . . Besides, I'd like to try it, to taste it. You're sure you haven't prepared any *Pon Mon* for us tonight? It's on the menu!"

The host decided to take the *Pon Mon* plunge. If they didn't like it; if their class, if their intellect won out, then he could always revert to his shon of the shoil claim.

"Um, yes, I have just a little *Pon Mon*. I fear that Nigerians will not have shoes or handbags so I get small *Pon Mon*."

He counted his guests. There were fourteen of them.

"I get fourteen pieces."

"Let's give it a try then," suggested Minister Alhaji Mustafa genially.

He actually had tried *Pon Mon* and had found it delicious as had the other guests, in their non-intellectual, non-governmental moments; which were many.

The *Pon Mon* was served; a piece a plate. The guests speared their forks into the cow skin and chewed. After much chewing, which is in the nature of eating *Pon Mon*—there were some dignified smackings of the tongue and a few delicate burps. Satisfaction was written on every face present. A lady, her head swathed in rich cloth said, "I have heard that it's the vogue abroad to wear cloth shoes. Velvet, satin . . . and the ladies use cloth handbags too. We really have no need for leather goods in this country."

"But what about briefcases ?" enquired the Minister sagely.

"Em, sah, velvet briefcase nice sah. It dey cover papers with velvet sah"

"Hmm" said the Minister "That settles it. I'll authourize a decree."

"The old decree banning *Pon Mon* sah…What go happen?"

"Haven't you heard of repeals?"

"Yes sah."

"It will be repealed. From now on *Pon Mon* will be authourized. It will be specifically, an upper class delicacy."

The host beamed, "*A la Pon Mon* sah"

"Precisely. *A la Pon Mon*!"

The shon of the shoil then disclosed that he had in fact

cooked a meal for *Pon Mon* eaters. He had known before with uncanny instinct that the future of Nigeria belonged to *Pon Mon* eaters.

There was an outburst of chatter. Nigerians wouldn't be poor if they allowed the eating of *Pon Mon*. Look at their host; this shon of the shoil. He had made his millions by being a shon of the shoil and by eschewing handbags for his wife and other leather goods throughout his life.

"But what about international opinion, sir? We can deal with our own Nigerian people and the legislation of eating *Pon Mon* but the outside world is another kettle of fish," warned the Minister of Externals.

Again there was an excited buzz of chatter until the host said humbly, "Kettle of fish sah. That is it."

"How so?"

"The Europeans cook fish for kettle and use same to make tea sah"

"And they get their tea from India and . . ."

"And the Americans get hot dog sah. They never consult Nigeria when they cook dog sah. It's a dog eat dog world sah."

"And they have lots of puddings in England like spotted dick and roly poly. And they didn't consult us about that either!"

"Given time *Pon Mon* will catch on, you'll see. We'll give it to the world."

"Look at those Indian restaurants. So many of them!"

"And the Chinese ones! Everyone has their own thing and is not afraid to promote it!"

"But when it's a Nigerian restaurant they always have continental dishes being served as well—as if the Nigerian ones are not enough."

"Anymore *Pon Mon*?"

"Sir do you think our cow population would mind? I mean being used exclusively for *Pon Mon*?" asked the woman with the turbaned head.

"Nonsense, you won't get a moo out of them!"

"So we're all agreed then, *Pon Mon* is to be institutionalized?"

The guests agreed and spent a happy evening chewing on their discussion and chewing the *Pon Mon*. And the shon of the shoil had yet another idea-- *a la Nigerian Pon Mon*—He said that it should be called by that name. That it should be served at Board Meetings and any institution where important discussions were scheduled to be held. This was because it could help in deliberations because of the chewing nature of *Pon Mon* which induced deep thought. Perhaps chewing gum could be outlawed and *Pon Mon* substituted . . .

The dinner continued far into the night. It only stopped when the chewing ended because that's when the *Pon Mon* ended.

As for the host, he became even wealthier with the establishment of *Pon Mon* delicatessens, and he also became a noted philosopher and intellectual—all because of his *Pon Mon*. But today he still calls himself "a shon of the shoil".

The Old Man

The phone calls began when her daughter was born. They began when she thought it was all over; the door of her bedroom creaking and announcing his entrance; the padded-old man-father-feet-soft-as-if-stalking-deliberate feet coming closer and closer still across the carpeted floor . . . until they reached the bed, her bed, and reached her, herself, with the sheets pulled up to her chin trying not to care; not to cry out.

He was her father, the old man. And before he uncovered her nine-year-old body (ten, eleven twenty or so) daughter-body he would always say, "Not to worry. Don't be afraid, my dear. It's only your old man."

Old man. Old man. The old man old . . . and it was her daughter's ninth birthday and the phone was ringing and she knew it was her father the old man on the line. On every and on each birthday of her daughter he had rung and she had re-lived the motions, her back resting on the chair, her back resting on the bed of her nine-year-old chair submitting to the old man's body above her and his voice which purred, "Don't be afraid. My dear, I am your old man."

"It's Grand-dad, isn't it, Mummy? He told me he would ring yesterday for my birthday, he told me . . . Mummy, why are you shivering? Grand-dad said you hate him because he's old and that's why we never go to see him at his house and that even when Grandma died you didn't go to the funeral and

89

he says he loves me and you hate him and I said . . ."

"Shut up. Do you hear me? Shut up! I told you never . . . never . . ."

But she was sobbing, her body shuddering; her back pressed against the bed of the chair, sobbing . . . and the ring-ring scream of the phone going on and on, rising and falling inside her and in her living room, this living room in which she sat with her daughter on her ninth birthday was her bedroom; the door creaking and announcing entrance of the old man all over again.

It was too late. Her daughter had picked up the phone, face flushed.

"No, don't! Don't . . .!"

"Thank you, Grand-dad . . . Yes, I'll try . . . and Grand-dad, I'll bring you some birthday cake."

And then her daughter sheepish, saying sorry Mummy but please pretty please Mummy please can we just go and see him this once for my birthday please and I'll be very good Mummy and he said he's very old now and that's why you call him the old man and he said he's so old that he can die at any time and he wants to see me before he dies please pretty please Mummy and if you agree that we can go and see him I'll just give him a little piece of cake, of my birthday cake, and Mummy you're always telling me to respect my elders and that . . . please Mummy for my birthday I've never ever asked you before and you said children should respect their elders and rev . . . reverence or something . . . .reverence them . . . don't you remember . . . please Mummy . . ."

Wearily she rose. Better go and see the old man now and get it over and done with, bury it, confront him. She was older, a married woman now with a nine-year-old daughter and she had told her child to respect and reverence her elders only two days before; that Africans, Nigerians, Yoruba's, respect their elders and a little girl does not run around half-naked when her father is in the house; and she had smacked her daughter, her anger wounding her daughter because Mummy had never smacked her before or said that just because they lived in genteel Victoria Island and didn't make her kneel to show respect for her parents and allowed children to look at grownups directly in the eyes, it didn't mean she could behave like that—run around half-naked—her father in the house.

Perhaps she was trying to make amends for the smacking, her angry outburst, her husband's amazed concern, her daughter's tears. Her daughter . . . perhaps . . .

"No, you don't need to say good-bye to your father. He's asleep in any case. Looks like you've cut a huge slice of cake for your Grand-dad," she said, feigning brightness.

She must put a stop to pretence today. Unlike her own mother who pretended it hadn't happened with the old man, she must put a stop to it, put a stop to pretence. She would confront her father today. He might be old; he was old but he was her father and she would confront him today and . . . .

But when she escorted her daughter to the car she felt her voice breaking.

"My dear," she said, helping to buckle up her daughter beside her in the car, "I'm only taking you to see your Grand-dad because . . ."

"Mummy, please be happy for me."

And she said nothing as her own mother had said nothing.

No. Her mother had said she should respect the old man, that he was wise, that he loved her and that she should never tell anyone if it was true which it wasn't and that if she should tell anyone then she would be smacked and that in any case no one would believe her and that she was trying to hurt her old man and disgrace their family and it wasn't true what she said and couldn't be. And then her mother had clasped her to herself and cried and cried.

"This is old Ikoyi," she said. "We'll soon be there and . . ."
"Yes, Mummy?"
"When you see your Grand-dad, don't . . . don't let him touch you, or kiss you, or anything."
"Mummy! So you really do hate him!"
"I'll allow you to be rude just this once. Calm down."

****

Curiously, the house looked much smaller than she remembered it. Could it have been so long ago when she ran? Packed her things and just ran? The gates were the same, though, iron topped with shards of glass jagging up into the air. And the silence of the grass with its flat stretch of green was the same, but the house was smaller. It seemed to have shrunk in size, its bungalow length reclining, the patio filled with cacti, their green and ochre up-thrusts of tubular lengths tufted with spikes and prickles. On that frenzy of night when she had run she had fallen over and the spikes had entered her flesh and now as she saw him she felt their scratch again. Now, though, when she saw the old man, she wondered at the fear she had felt when he entered and told her not to be afraid and not to cry out—for now he was shrunken and he was really an old man. Old man, her mother had said she should call him. To make things easier, her mother had said. Her mother had said, "To make it hurt less, make it easier, think of him as the old man." It was the only time her mother had directly referred to what the old man did for so many nights of her childhood she had lost count.

His frame was emaciated and fragile and his voice quavered. Avoiding her eyes, he embraced his grand-daughter and she followed as he led them across the patio and into the house.

"Thank you, thank you, my dear, for coming. I'm so old now, so many illnesses it would fill a book to recount them. I can die at any moment and I so wanted to see my grand-daughter. What a lovely girl! As lovely as you were at her age. I can die at any moment and I so wanted to see my grand-daughter. Thank you for coming"

She gazed around and tried to overlook her daughter's sitting on the old man's knees.

"We'll have some of that birthday cake, yes?" said the old man.

"With drinks! And my Mummy likes tea with no sugar or milk."

"Ah! So she still likes that, yes. Yes. But before we settle down, my dear grand-daughter, I want to take you around . . . I want to take you in the garden, and show you the flowers. I've been doing a lot of gardening since your dear grand-mother died. I've been planting lots of cacti too . . ."

"Mummy won't mind; it's my birthday. You don't mind, do you, Mummy?"

She didn't mind. The old man was going to give his grand-daughter a walk through the garden and the garden is outdoors and the garden is without doors which creak in the silence of the night. There are no beds in the garden.

Leaving their chatter without a word she left them; and she walked around the house opening door after door looking in. Here is the kitchen, austere and white in the sunlight. Here is the old man's study with its neat books—covers, really, for they were for decoration only and hollow inside. And here was her mother's room, a squeeze of silence covered in dust with a single bed which she had taken to sleeping in alone; and not with the old man soon after her mother had embraced daughter and had told her nothing had happened. And here is the old man's room with its cupboards and wardrobes and his many suits and *agbadas*, for he liked to dress with style, his clothing matching. Even his pyjamas had matching dressing gowns, he changed them every time he came, he had many pyjamas and she remembered his fingers tugging at his pyjamas. And here at the end, the last room, used to be . . . here . . . nothing had changed. And she whispered, "Nothing has changed."

She kicked off her shoes and lay on the bedcover. It smelt of mildew and must. Getting up she pulled back the bedcover, the sheets, and curled up in the bed and her heart began to beat, to beat, for it was night-time again for her nine-year-old-daughter-self and the door began its wheezing creak like an old man's cough wheezing and short of breath and she heard soft-father-padding-old-man-father-steps entering; and in a rush she thought of her daughter. It was her ninth birthday, her daughter's and hers, sounding in her mind. "Nothing has changed."

Nothing. No thing has changed. Her heart was expanding and she ripped the bedclothes from her bed of nine years old, ten, eleven, twenty-some years . . . running out of the room with its door . . . past the rooms and out of the door running into the garden so fast that she nearly collided with a pot of cacti.

Where were they? Her daughter. The old man. Where were they? To which part of the garden had they gone, which lying bed where hot gasps and up and down movement above her tore at her insides. Where? Would the cacti prickly and flesh-green-upright know? Would the bungalow with its reclining length of looking on know?

The old man . . . his arm around his grand-daughter, and they were moving closer, closer still, and when she sobbed, her naked tears swelling with hurt, the old man came to her, touched her timidly, his voice a drawl which lingered around her, wrapping around her like a disused old bandage covering a throbbing wound.

And in the drawl she heard rebuke; it was a teasing drawl of rebuke. "My daughter, what did you think? What were you thinking? You look frightened! Did you think I was . . . I am your old man, yes, but she . . ."

The old man squeezed his grand-daughter's hand "This little girl is my grand-daughter and besides . . . besides, I am too old for that, now."

The Wedding Cake Plot

The guests, and even the bridegroom and even the Nigerian environment and even her parents - in fact, absolutely everyone and everything who attended Deola's wedding reception - watched her with undisguised, unrestrained, un-knowledgeable horrified horror.

Never before in the marital historical records of Nigerian, Ikoyi, Victoria Island or, indeed, world history, they were sure, had a newly wedded wife behaved in such a violent manner; rushing into the kitchen of her parent's house returning with a vicious carving knife in her hand…and…and in such luxurious surroundings too.

The wedding itself had been conducted at Deola's request in her parent's wide garden; with its specially imported willow trees, their leaves dripping gracefully to the specially dug lake; the leaves of the willow trees were so graceful and so elegantly leaved and the trunks of the willow trees were so supine and slimly tree trunked that the regular Nigerian palms; the potted ones and the ones who towered right up to the roof of the sky began to feel somewhat insecure when they saw the English willow trees; when they heard the famed opera singer and psychiatrist, Mr. Armani Gucci, singing a song of beautiful willow trees with a voice as sweet as a willow full of psychological meaning and intent.

For a while all went smoothly, and they forgot to feel

insecure when they saw Deola and her bridegroom; the couple looked splendid as did their bridal retinue. Deola stood out in her three flounced white satin wedding dress; and she was surrounded by hundreds of bridesmaids dressed in candy pink floss gowns; their arms and backs bared the modern way; and the hundreds of groom's men were dressed in spruce suits, white shirts and from their several throats dangled striped pink ties; like the bridesmaids they wore white gloves. They were a spectacle to behold when Deola took her vows.

Being a modern Nigerian woman, as she took care to impress upon as many who would listen; Deola had told her friends and relatives and just about everyone, that at the wedding reception, she would give a surprise speech which was up her wedding sleeve even though of course being bare backed Deola's wedding dress had no discernible sleeves.

"The time for my surprise speech has come," she announced and she smiled.

Since there was no obvious reaction she repeated the words rather loudly; in fact, so loudly that even the English willow trees shook some of their leaves into the specially dug lake.

"The time for my surprise speech has come," Deola repeated. "I am now a married woman. See that wedding cake over there," she said, pointing at the wedding cake at the far end of the garden, "it's a modern wedding cake and it was brought to Nigeria by my friend, Mr. Armani Gucci, who is famed for his grainy willowy erudition of songs to do with trees. I saw his name on the internet and contacted him. He's interested in women like me and when I told him of the wedding he agreed to come for this modern wedding and sing for us which he has done very well. I could hardly stop crying when I heard him sing so sweetly. Now to the main point of my speech…by the way, thanks everyone for attending my wedding. My husband has agreed that rather than the custom of the husband making a speech, I'm the one who will make it. Basically I want you lot to know that neither my husband nor anyone else is going to saddle me with societal expectations of becoming a mother. Just because I am now a married woman doesn't mean I want to be a mother. As you know I don't care for children that much. I will not be subjected to the Yoruba custom of being called "Mama this" or "Mama that" if I do decide to have children. I'm a modern Nigerian woman and bride. I want to make that absolutely clear."

A huge gasp escaped from every single mouth of the crowd.

But Deola was nonplussed.

"Besides, I'm a career woman as you all know," Deola continued. "I have already started a cake business. I will be specializing in wedding-cakes."

Another gasp escaped the crowd. And the guests began to look sideways at Deola's parents who according to Deola's dictates were dressed in blue suits; because she said she'd discovered from her 'journeys' on the internet, that people in modern Western countries, particularly "the bride's mum" were expected to wear blue at weddings.

Deola's mother was decidedly blue at this point and she hung her head down low. And another very huge silence followed for what seemed like forever to Deola's mother. But Deola's father felt that if he laughed, others would laugh and the embarrassment of the family would be drowned in laughter, so he laughed loudly. It worked and soon everyone and everything, including the willow trees and the specially dug lake, were laughing.

And with that somewhat boisterous laughter surrounding her, Deola's discomfiture became evident. Tears jumped from her eyes because even her bridegroom couldn't stop himself from laughing . . . so this was Deola's surprise speech? She must be joking; she was obviously joking; and he looked at her face and laughed some more . . . he hadn't known that she was such a good actress. But wait a minute; those were real tears in her eyes! Dear Deola so independent and modern and yet she's crying like every other woman over nothing. When they began their life together as a married couple; as husband and wife he would encourage her to stop this female crying thing . . . thank heavens, she has stopped crying. Just as well; it's time for the cutting of the cake.

Yes Deola had stopped crying and it was time for the ceremonial cutting of the cake; but with her hand held up dismissively Deola asked the crowd to remain where they were including her new husband. She seemed to be drawn to the Wedding Cake by an invisible power.

And along with the crowd and the Nigerian environment and of course the imported willow trees and specially dug lake, Deola's new husband watched her march towards a table at the far end of the garden; on which a Wedding Cake sat surrounded by roses, lilies and daffodils on a tablecloth made of the finest Belgian lace.

Although the wedding cake had been laced with several cups of brandy and various liquors it was not drunk in the least. In fact, the Wedding Cake had been listening to Deola's every word. And the Wedding Cake decided to speak to

Deola in cake language. And so in cake language it spoke with several spokes.

"Deola" the wedding cake said:
Get this into your head.
In case you haven't heard I'm a man
Male grain patriarch- ally directed
A man dressed up to look like a woman
Haven't you noticed that your wedding dress tiers, your flounces
Your bows and your bounces
Mirror my three tier flounces
My bows and my bounces?

To the astonishment of all, Deola stood still, frozen on the spot, her ears listening to the wedding cake's words, which continued with relentless relent its wedding cake jabs:

Deola you spurn my significance
With female shenanigans
Going against the grain
I'm made from fertile reproductive inducing grain.

The audience, for by now they had become an audience as opposed to mere wedding guests; gazed at a dazed Deola who was looking down at her belly. She turned in the direction of where the Wedding Cake sat with pretended matronly content and heard the wedding cake say in a voice not-so-nice:

By the way, Deola, Mr. Rice
Knows this wedding cake plot
We're both grain you see
Our intention being to induce you into reproductivity

That's why rice is thrown on women after the marriage ceremony
Your purpose as woman is the marital bed
And that alone
To produce and reproduce children
Without any choice of your own
Have you got that you stupid modern Western so called thinking
Nigerian bride?

Clearly the wedding cake was not on Deola's side. And by this time, Deola was walking with slow thoughtful steps around and around the Wedding Cake but he acted as if he didn't care; he actually didn't care what Deola thought; not a jot and continued:

Nigerian modern or not
From Ancient Roman times brides
Had their heads covered in biscuit like crumbs
Made from flour and grain fecundity
For a certain reproductive reproduction fluidity
Before and for after in the marital bed

In 1648 Robert Herrick
First conceived true purpose
Of me Wedding Cake
I've been baked to encourage female fertility
That's my grain ability
And Deola—

To the astonishment of her audience, Deola, minus her white flounces of wedding gown, stooped to take off her white shoes. She hurried past the cake and entered the house proper.

What was she up to? What on earth had come over her?

Deola soon re-appeared, a carving knife in her hand and with the sight of it the spell was broken as in a body all of the guests ran towards her. And what they saw on Deola's face shocked them not a little but a lot actually. Deola's face was covered in streams of modern, mostly modern female tears, and the tears were shaped like the leaves of the imported willow trees; and the tears flowed down to what looked like a newly dug mouth which looked like a lake; and Deola's normally pretty face seemed to be transformed into an inter-netting map of the world with nose and cheek mountains and eyes of oceans and lands of honed skin and the entire map of her face was being drawn continually by an invisible hand and the hand was a male hand...perhaps, perhaps not...they weren't sure.

They were many conflicting reports of the event of Deola and the Wedding Cake which continue to feature in the gossip columns of many a Nigerian daily, monthly and yearly. The audience were not quite sure what they saw on Deola's face that day. . . what they were certain about was that knife in Deola's hands.

Deola was stabbing the wedding cake viciously in rapid succession and then dropped the carving knife after a while. Deola then threw the pieces of wedding cake to the ground and stomped on each piece until her distraught new husband broke free from the crowd and hugged his sobbing bride.

The preparations, the wedding, the reception, her speech, her importation of the willow trees and her desire to have that artificial lake constructed for their wedding day had all but unhinged her.

Deola's new husband clasped her in his arms but she drew away from him and was shouting and screaming at the wedding cake.

"All your pretence. You, you stupid Wedding Cake!" she screamed hugging herself close.

Deola was immediately taken to the hospital and has spent several years in therapy for what became known as The Wedding Cake Murder. Deola is still uncertain whether she did murder a wedding cake or whether a wedding cake murdered her.

When the many visitors, including Mr. Armani Gucci, come to see Deola in the hospital, saying that that particular wedding cake was such an exquisite work of craftsmanship, a veritable masterpiece of cake-making and how could Deola behave like that at her own wedding and could she not just snap out of this modern fandangle nonsense about not wanting children and not wanting to be called Mama this and Mama that...her poor husband...her poor parents...Deola sobs, and tears roll down her cheeks. She looks at her tears to see if they are shaped like grains and if they feel grainy. But they're not. Her tears are real tears; but she is sceptical about everything now...since that wretched wedding cake debacle she questions everything even her tears...are the tears she feels coursing down her cheeks part of a monstrous grain patriarchal engendered wedding cake plot?

Commercialized Palm Wine

Commercial was what she was and had become. Curvy and tall and clad in see through bottle green and labelled. She had the same label as her sister. There was dry palm wine and sweet palm wine and they shared the same label. On the label a picture of tradition with a palm wine tapster climbing a palm tree trunk.

The tree itself as tall and slender as her commercialized sister on the bottle; the head of the tree a toss of graceful green hair blowing over the tapster as he climbed. The tapster securely attached to the trunk of the tree by means of a rope. Tap tapping to unleash the gush of white froth of liquid potent which could make you drunk if you weren't careful about your tapping and your drinking.

Nigerian bottling authorities had decided to make palm wine commercial; so much easier to deal with than the old traditional way of waiting for your own personal tapster to come to your yard; waiting for him to tie the rope around his waist, connect himself to the tree trunk, climb the tree, tap the tree for its' palm wine and pour it into calabashes.

So much easier, this bottle already filled with palm wine. Go to the supermarket. Exchange money for bottle. The bottle bought and you have the palm wine in a bottle. All that tradition of palm wine now thankfully poured into this easy bottle.

Tradition . . . my neighbour downstairs, an Igbo man, said that even today, when a woman is about to choose her husband, she gives him a sip of palm wine. Singles him out as her man, kneels before him and he sips her palm wine and that sip means that their marriage is sealed.

I'd seal my own commitment to my husband in my own way with a beef dish marinated, the meat marinated in palm wine from this bottle.

I'd already cut up chunks of meat, seasoned them, and now it was time to open the bottle of palm wine and pour it over the meat and let it stand for a couple of hours before proceeding with the cooking. My husband, when he arrived after his travels would be delighted. Any man would be. I had invented a new dish just like the Nigerian manufacturers of bottled palm wine had invented the bottled variety. But I couldn't open the bottle. And my *oyinbo* foreigner heart skipped several beats I can tell you.

Not because I couldn't open the bottle. It was what happened when I went downstairs to get help to open my bottle that trouble came. Even now I can hardly believe the friction; my embarrassment.

My neighbour's wife was returning to Lagos on the same plane as my husband; and thinking myself respectful in view of our age difference; in view of our gender difference; in view of our marital status—in full view you must understand—I had always, no matter the circumstance of my visits while our spouses were away- indulged in a little chit chat before getting down to business. I was thoroughly Nigerianized you see. If I went into a bank or a supermarket where the staff knew me, we would talk about the weather, the economy, ask after our respective families or health before actually proceeding with business.

So when I went upstairs to my neighbour's flat I indulged in traditional chit chat for a while. Then I told him the purpose of my visit.

"Sir, I'm in a bit of a tizzy."

His eyebrows rose good-humouredly and I extracted the bottle of palm wine from my bag.

"Could you please help me to open this bottle of palm wine?"

He was silent.

"Please" I said, thrusting the bottle into his hands.

He looked at me and then traced the label with a long thinking ascertaining finger.

"So this is the new commercial bottle of palm wine I've been hearing about?"

Why doesn't he just get an opener and open the bottle?

"Can you, will you?" I ask with as much respect as I can muster.

He holds the body of the bottle tight and sits down in one of his armchairs. He hasn't even told me to have a seat.

Why has this woman come here, to my house yet again? Can't she get someone else to open this palm wine bottle for her? And to think her husband and my wife are coming in tonight on the plane . . . She's even dressed in the same green colour as the bottle; a slinky green dress; more like a slip than a dress; showing up her curves.

"Is anything the matter? Sorry to press but I'm in a hurry. You know my husband and your wife are on the . . ."

"Yes," he agrees, "I know. They're on the same plane."

He settles himself in the chair and shouts "So this is the new bottle of palm wine!"

This is probably some kind of African cultural thing. But why doesn't he just go to the kitchen and get the opener? I must try to be patient.

"Nice label," he announces.

Why on earth is he staring at my body like that?

She says she wants me to open this bottle of palm wine and then presumably we will have a drink, toast each other and then get drunk and then what? There's that label. The palm wine tapster climbing and tapping his tree and the palm tree with so much leafy hair. Like her hair.

He's making no attempt to go to the kitchen for the opener. Maybe I should just go there myself and get the damn thing.

She's looking around the apartment as if she's never been here before. What is the world coming to? She is a married woman and I am a married man. And our spouses are expected this very night.

"I don't like opening wine bottles, palm wine bottles, bottles of any kind. It's not, it's not proper"

Not proper?

A smile is on the edge of his lips and it looks as if it is about to fall over; this smile.

"But why not? I really need you to open it before my husband comes. It can't wait. I can't wait."

What is wrong with this man? He can open bottles. I know he can. I've even seen him doing so with his teeth. Perhaps he wants me to kneel before him and ask him respectfully.

"I don't care for palm wine," he mutters.

And he gets out of his chair and he goes to the far corner of the room and looks through the window.

"But I've seen you drinking many times."

This woman can be persistent. She thinks I don't know her game. There are only a few hours to go before our spouses return and she comes to my flat in a silky green dress and asks me to open a bottle of palm wine.

"Why don't you wait until your husband returns, then he will be able to open your bottle of palm wine. I've given up all forms of alcohol, and if I drink at all, it's only in the company of my wife. And we both know she's expected any moment."

Has this man, this neighbour, gone out of his mind? How will I be able to marinate the beef in time with all this 'I can't do this' and 'I won't do that?'

I move towards him. He is still holding the bottle of palm wine tightly.

"Please," I say, "I'm desperate. We're running out of time. I don't want my husband, your wife to catch us."

He stands stiff.

Some females are impossible. I can't believe this. She comes to my house, visits my house in my wife's absence and her own husband's absence at all times of the day, to have a chat she says. And this was leading up to…Does she think she can seduce me so easily?

"Why do you want me to open the bottle?"

I'd better kneel now; and get this traditional shindig thing out of the way. And so I move to the other side of the room and kneel before him so he knows; just so he knows, I mean business.

"Please Oga, I want to prepare a beef dish in the wine…there's very little time."

Desperate. She's desperate. Another opportunity like this just might not arise. Both of our spouses are away. There's very little time she says; very little time. Soon she'll be saying she'll cook for me. It's a wonder she hasn't tried this ploy before now. And she's kneeling, just like my wife kneeled for me when she chose me; for marriage. My wife chose me. Now this oyinbo . . . this foreigner . . . she's acting like a prostitute . . . it's all over her . . .

And I'm on my feet.

He looks at me, the bottle of palm wine, and starts to describe the picture on the label.

"I see the tapster is tapping wine from the tree."

"Of course he is," I say, "What else do tapsters do? Will you or won't you open the bottle? They'll be home soon. I wanted you to . . ."

"I know, I know. But it's not right."

"What's not right? They've probably landed now and it will take them about half an hour to get through immigration, customs, and get their baggage and then another hour for them to drive home. There's still time."

This is strange. One would think that if she could have held out for so many weeks when her husband was away, then another few hours would not be too much to ask. This is really quite shocking.

"You're a calculating woman aren't you?"

"What do you mean I'm a calculating woman?"

"You've got everything well worked out down to the last second, haven't you?"

"I suppose I have. When you're a woman and in the business of cooking and preparing meals, you have to ascertain time or else . . ."

"That's what I mean by your being calculating."

This man is ridiculous. First he says he doesn't know how to open bottles which is a lie. Then he says he only drinks when he is with his wife. Another lie. I wonder what his next excuse will be? I might as well abandon the idea of cooking beef in palm wine; my new recipe. Perhaps it's too new a recipe to try; he's giving me the look over.

He hands me the bottle of palm wine and he shouts: "No I won't !"

"That's all you needed to say!"

Now she's pretending to be the injured party. One has to be on one's guard with women. Always up to their tricks to get you to do what you don't want to do. They will come to your house, alone, in anything they choose to wear and pretend that they want a simple conversation, and then, before you know it, it's 'Please open this bottle of palm wine ' Does she think I'm stupid ? And who ever heard of beef soaked in palm wine? It's not our tradition.

She's going to the door.

And about time.

"I'm sorry," he says, "But I simply won't be party to this whim of yours!"

"Whim!" I shriek, "I've been thinking about this ever since my husband left the country."

The audacity. These women and their concoctions. A devious crew. I wonder what tack she would have taken if palm wine had not been commercialized? Why, they even call some of these women commercial workers nowadays.

He's actually grinning.

My hand on the door knob...

"Another time...Another time perhaps," he says closing the supercilious door behind me.

In my flat I look at the bottle of palm wine with its label. I guess I won't be able to cook the beef in the palm wine. And if I do buy palm wine again I'll have to make sure that it has the right sort of label. Or, better still, no label whatsoever. But then again I'm a woman and I've been labelled as such already. Perhaps I should give up cooking. But then again I might be labelled a man for not executing my wifely duties. Then again…

The Hart and The Hound

It was such a cold shivering cold winter. Pedestrians walked quickly along the pavement; bent double, bracing the harsh cold wind; their coverings of thick drape of coats, hats pulled down over faces; scarves strangling necks; mufflers cramped over ears; hands gloved or shoved into pockets...bodies all; bodies attempting to gather some warmth which there was none...there was no warmth it seemed to him anywhere on this Oxford pavement in winter; no brightness, no colour; and he wondered where these people walking beside him, their bodies bent over double and their down faces down...he wondered where these people were going to and when they got there if the cold would leave them if they entered their houses warm; and removed their winter covering of clothes ; if they left this cold chill; like a death imprisoning them as he felt imprisoned . . . he wondered if, when they arrived at their destinations whether they would feel the warmth he could not feel.

It seemed like a scene from a Lowry painting to him; he was in a wide grey sky canvas of match stick men disembodied by their covering; trying their very best to assert some kind of self in this awful cold with their hurrying boot-booted feet attempting to move, to leave this-that painting; but they were trapped and static even as they walked ; drained of colour; trapped as he felt trapped.

He too wanted to get out of the cold and that pub on the corner might be a good place to get some shelter. He needed some warmth inside him and a meal and a drink . . . that pub at the corner beckoned; he had never been there before. He had been warned by the few English student friends he had managed to make, to avoid the place.

Yes you're a student in our country and yes you're doing your D.Phil but . . . how can we put it? That pub, The Hart and Hound doesn't take kindly to strangers of your sort.

Strangers of my sort?

He had never ventured there; gone to The Hart and Hound; it was for the locals they said. Stick to other restaurants and pubs.

Didn't you hear what that Enoch Powell bloke said on the radio and the tele?

He was nearing the corner and the pub and there was no point in returning to his lodgings and it was beginning to snow; he had been told that when it snowed warmth would come; but he felt the chill air eating away inside him . . . no there was no point in returning to his flat; the heating system was not working as it should.

Perhaps it was because he was Nigerian that even when he turned the heating thermostat all the way up; even with the double glazing windows . . . in spite of all that he still felt the chill of winter entering his bones.

Better to just go into this pub; order a meal, some wine and get some warmth; then it would be bed and he would be able to face another cold day. The winter with its cold and its short days of sunlight couldn't last forever could it?

He felt unaccountably depressed; with this season, in this season of so little light. He could never get used to it. It was so unlike Nigeria with its hot brazen sun which always seemed to shine even when there was no visible sun; even in the rainy season or during the Harmattan when the winds blew from over the Sahara desert and settled itself on trees, bushes, houses, everything in a dust covering, like another kind of snow; but that covering of snow could be removed with ease; it wasn't like the snow here which was light as flimsy dust but which gathered and gathered again covering the world of the city and the world in white. He must be homesick. This feeling of depression entering him with its gnawing coldness must be because he was homesick.

Yes he would enter The Hart and Hound standing there on the corner. He turned up his coat collar and walked rapidly bent double trying not to fall . . . the pavement was so slippery . . . Momentarily he paused to look at the pub's emblem. The wind must have torn away its covering; he had not seen it before and looking at it he shuddered. Set against a white sky and framed in a heart shape of gilded gold colouring, there was a painting of a deer, the hart, pursued and running; the hart was fixed but running in wide eyed flight from the hound behind it. The hound's sleek body with its' large head, its' red slobbering lips; the boils of saliva delicate drawn circles, beneath the lips of the hound as it pursued the hart; the hound's tail upright and on the way to a triumphant wag and wagging as it went in for the kill . . . .

But when he entered the pub, hearing its tinkling bell behind him, announcing his entrance; the interior was a comfort of warmth. Despite the shock of silence in raised eyebrows and looks as he went in; it was a comfort of warmth. And deliberately he put out of his mind the warnings against coming to this pub; and the warnings said and unsaid in the

Enoch Powell speech which made him shiver more than the cold of winter . . . rivers of blood, Powell had said . . . if the blacks of our colonies don't go back to where they came from . . . the streets will flow; be covered with rivers of blood . . . the blacks would be hounded out . . . rivers of blood . . .

The pub was full; resumption of talk and laughter; the chink of glasses and the sound of cutlery on plates as he walked down the red carpeted length of parting; parting the separate sides of the room with their booths of intimacy on either side of the room he focused on the bar at the far end of the pub; shelves of liquor in bottles curved and straight. Glasses and beer mugs neatly arranged . . . and as he walked towards the bar he could see a man, ginger haired, wiping a glass chatting with someone and the someone sat by an empty stool and the someone had a back and the back was wearing a flimsy looking blouse; and that surprised him; that in this cold weather the back wore next to nothing. Brown hair straggled onto its shoulders. And even before he sat on the stool beside the back and beside her he knew that his stopping on the way to this pub; the Hart and Hound was no accident. His depression had melted with the sight of her back. It was a vulnerable wanting back; a back which said it wanted to connect with him back; and it said it openly and nakedly with its flimsy blouse. He felt warmth in that back; he wanted to touch it and enfold the body attached to the back in his arms.

"This pub is for us locals," said the bar tender appraising him.

"Give over Ed. It's freezing outside! And he doesn't look as if he comes from these parts," exclaimed the woman with the back. "Where are you from love?" she said turning to him.

"Nigeria. I'm a student at Balliol College."

Ed frowned. "Student eh? What tribe are you?"

"Tribe?"

"Yeah you blackies belong to tribes don't you? Are you Zulu? Seen a film once on a big black warrior bloke. Name was Chaka Zulu or something."

"That would be South Africa. I'm from Nigeria."

"He was a big bloke was Chaka Zulu. Big and black like you and he had a cutlass or something in his hand. All of the blackies in that film did but they were no match for us Brits!"

"Oh for Christ's sake Ed! Give the man a drink. Why do you have to question him like that?" asked the woman beside him; and he looked at her face. And the same vulnerability he saw in her back was in her face with its wide deer like desperate innocent eyes; its pinched nose and those freckles spattered on either side of the nose . . . as if they wanted to merge into a solid colour but didn't know how quite to do it. Her chin was a dainty pointed thing and her skin was as transparent as fine white paper; paper which could be so easily torn it made his blood rush with the wanting to protect her from a something he could not define; a something he knew not what.

But it was there in her; in her body and in the way her eyes darted as if she was being pursued.

"Do people stare like you're staring in Nigeria?" she asked and began to tear away with deliberate precise fingers at the fish on the plate before her. She grabbed a bottle of thick red tomato sauce and poured it over the fish and chips.

"Fish and chips," she muttered. "Best meal in the world I always say. Are you staring because of this here tomato sauce or what? I likes to eat everything with a good old dollop of tomato sauce; even bread!"

Ed watched them, his fingers drumming the counter.

"What do you want Chaka Zulu? Why have you come to The Hart and Hound?"

"Give him fish and chips and a pint," said the woman. "What's your name love?"

But he was mesmerized; not only by the way she tore at the fish flesh and chewed the slivers in her mouth; and the way she poured the tomato sauce over her food after each mouthful; he was fascinated by her hunger, a ravenous hunger; and he was entranced all the more; he wouldn't have expected a woman with a back like hers and a face like hers to eat with such . . . he couldn't think of the word . . . relish, yes relish . . . that was the word.

He continued to watch her not trying to hide the intensity of his stare. She had not touched the crinkly golden chips on her plate but was concentrating on the fish and she was eating with her fingers; the wrapped up fork and knife, abandoned, wrapped up in a paper napkin; and he could see the blade of the knife and the prongs of the fork peeping through the napkin's covering.

He hadn't seen any English person in a restaurant, anywhere-- eating with their hands before.

"You're giving me the chills looking at me like that," she said, "And I've had enough bother for one day. Haven't you got fish and chips where you come from in Nigeria? You still haven't told me your name and you still haven't told Ed what you want to eat!"

He turned his gaze to Ed, the bar tender and that painting . . .

"Is that a Lowry I see on the wall?"

"Lowry? What the hell is Lowry? It's just a painting! Chaka Zulu what'd you want? I haven't got all day!"

"I think I'll just have a drink please."

Ed feigned a yawn, "And what drink would that be if you don't mind me asking Chaka Zulu?"

"My name is John."

"John?" asked the woman.

"Yes, John."

"But that's an English name ain't it? How come you're Nigerian and you've got an English name?"

"We were colonized by the British."

"You what?"

"Chaka Zulu what do you want to drink? I'm a busy man. I haven't got . . . Sal give over with that ketchup can't you? Wouldn't be surprised if that's why Bill called it quits with you!"

"And who are you to tell the whole world my business Ed? Bill didn't have much going for him anyways. Unemployed and a right bastard when he got drunk which is everyday. Ed serve John here before I get a heart attack!"

And John saw her reaching yet again for the bottle of tomato sauce; pour-pouring its red ooze over the chips.

"Chaka what'll you have?"

John ordered red wine.

"Bordeaux 1997 if you've got it," he said surveying the rows of bottles before him.

"So Chaka wants Bordeaux 1977 if you've got it," muttered Ed moving away to a door leading into an interior room.

"Don't mind Ed. He's an alright bloke. So do you like Oxford John? You must be very clever. Best university in the world isn't it? I'm not that educated me self. Is it too cold for you here? I never feels the cold. I expects I'd like to live in a hot country though. My name's Sal by the way; short for Sally.

Sally Dickinson. What's your other name John?" she asked sticking her red fingers into her mouth and sucking them.

Ordinarily he would have been repulsed but that same vulnerability in her back; her face, her edgy on the edge voice and those freckles of longing to be just one which spattered across her cheekbones . . . all of it charmed him; charmed him inexplicably.

"Well I don't know if you'll be able to pronounce my name," he demurred, "but since you ask Sal . . . it's John Ogunkoya".

She repeated the name softly, "John Ogunkoya. Why it's lovely. Sounds like a song it does John Ogunkoya. You're good news on a bad day. I didn't like Bill anyways. Are you married John Ogunkoya? I hear you Africans have loads of wives but I know that's all prejudiced bull shit isn't it?"

No, he told her; he was not married.

Ed was approaching, in his hand a bottle of red wine.

"Couldn't get the year you wanted. Will this do Chaka?' he said pouring the wine into a beer mug.

"Don't you have any wine glasses in this pub?"

"Look here Chaka blackie!" . . . and an angry tomato-red flush stained Ed's cheeks. He was trembling; and all of a sudden the talk, the chatter, the laughter, everything seemed to stop with that shout in the pub. And the cold which John had, he thought left outside came to him with that shout and that silence.

John rose and walked down the red carpet and past the silent booths of the pub with their red velvet upholstered chairs; the studied gold studs gleaming like a crowd of small gold eyes, as he walked to the door of the pub and heard its tinkling bell tinkling behind him.

Outside the cold air slamming his face down to the cobbled slate of grey pavement; the pressing weight of the sky falling on his bent head…he was not sure how he felt. It was too cold to feel anything. And it was snowing. His coat wasn't thick enough and his shoes…he had not heeded the weather forecast warnings and had not dressed up warmly enough for the cold of this day. He shivered. He would catch a bad cold…

"John! John Ogunkoya!"

It was that woman from the pub, Sal. He stopped and half turned and watched her struggling to prevent herself from slipping. If she did have a coat or a jacket she wasn't wearing it; she had been upset for him and had run out of the pub to comfort him; and his heart went out to her again. He smiled as she came towards him. And when she was beside him and he saw her face and the tears in her eyes like perfect drawn circles of melting snow; he held her close and he did not feel the cold. He unbuttoned his coat and she snuggled into it; and it was so very cold but he did not feel the cold.

In his flat he asks her why she is so serious. He tries to make her laugh and asks her if she wants some thick red tomato sauce on her biscuits and in her tea.

"Well you know Bill and I split. But that's not the whole of it. That's not why I've been down . . . ."

"You're killing me with all of this suspense," he says.

" O. K. John Ogunkoya. I just lost me job."

"What's your job?"

"They call us care givers"

"I kind of expected that Sally; that you'd be a care giver. What happened? How did you lose your job?"

"Promise you won't laugh?"

"Why on earth would I laugh because a beautiful woman who has helped me in so many ways has lost her job?"

"We both know I'm not beautiful. Goodness it's really hot in here. Is this what it's like in Africa? I've always wanted to experience really hot weather."

"Tell me how you lost your job Sal."

John watches as she removes her flimsy blouse, her long skirt, her shoes; as she walks around the sitting room and looks at his TV, his stereo set, his many books in their book shelves.

"It's true! You African blokes are really rich . . . well at least the ones who come over here to the UK as students. I've never seen so many books in me life and that stereo system you've got must have cost you a pretty penny . . . why do you keep the place so hot John?"

"Why can't you tell me how . . . why you lost your job Sal?"

"John I lost me job because a Nigerian woman . . . she's got more education than me and I was only a temp anyways. Anyways she got me job at Radcliffe Infirmary. It won't be easy to get a job because of that blackie. But I'm O.K. I'm really O.K."

John says he is sorry.

"I confess I wanted to do her in at first. Blacks coming in from our colonies to the UK and taking our jobs...everything. I confess I wanted to do her in, that woman. She's so uppity. I wanted to do her in and watch her blood running all over the floor. When that blackie woman sees me eating fish and chips with me hands and pouring tomato sauce and all she says to me, she says, I'm lower class, she says. And she a blackie! I thinks to me self what's the world coming to when a blackie gets to lording it over you as if you're the scum of the earth? But when you John comes into the pub and I see how that idiot

Ed talks to you and you don't say nothing but walks out . . . I likes your humility and your dignity John Ogunkoya. I likes your class. You're a classy bloke you are John Ogunkoya. I've heard say that Chaka Zulu toffs are all over Nigeria. And when I sees you ordering that Border wine thing like the gentleman you are John Ogunkoya, I says to myself I've found me an African prince. You're a prince aren't you John Ogunkoya? Why I bet you've never even had fish and chips. Not to talk less of covering over everything with good old tomato sauce. You don't like stuff that's covered do you John?"

John feels cold. When he sees her nakedness, her wide deer eyes running around the room his heart breaks. He wants her to cover herself up; he wishes he had never seen her vulnerable back; he wants to run; and he wishes...he wishes he did not feel so very trapped-wound-hounded. The day is so very cold.

Picnic At Epe

Should you dig deep into the dark bowelled earth and wrench an onion from the root; and hold its circumference in the cup of your palm—your skin will be skin-startled by the bald nakedness of its shiny smooth in the centre of your palm, obscuring life-line etched dark-deep in hand-skin.

From the earth where it has lain in germinating burial; smothered where it has earth been in shrouds of layers upon layers of translucent skin in the cup of your hand; as it is in my hand; a small round head in my hand without eyes, nose; without mouth or ears in my hands it is; And it is – It is perfect picnic fare.

In the writings which treat this not so vegetable roundness delved from earth, warnings are sounded. Precautionary measures advised. They say that when you cut-cut it and when you peel-peel it, layer after layer—place a slice of bread between your lips in prevention of the acrid fumes which shout pain and cause tears to sprout from your dark-grounded eyes. The bread will be barrier-bread absolving tears and you will not cry. It is the only vegetable which can cause you to shed unwanted tears. Use your head. Deny your senses. Be alive to unwanted tears. Place bread-barrier between your lips. The warnings of hidden tears and tearing tears are then blocked-barriered in its roundness of onion head.

Not many Africans know about the in-held hurt- spurt-tearing tears of an onion. This African Diasporan knows; and knows and knows but did not know until the picnic; at Epe. She knows of the pain of the wrenching from dark earth. Of the nakedness; life-line obscured, and burials in land and of sea crossing crossings. Burials she knows of in new lands wrenched from the root. This African Diasporan also knows as I know now of this; this other warning. No bread precautions threading my lips.

I slice this onion; knife-slice it with cutting edge of knife in rounds. We are going for a picnic at Epe. And I slice this onion, coating its rings in batter, and frying them. It is perfect picnic fare for a picnic at Epe.

That's where it began and ended and began again. Epe. It is a village on the outskirts of Lagos. It is a sleepy sloth of place buried under a hot dazing sun, the Atlantic sea limping beside it; languishing in a long laze of innocence which beguiles visitors. There is a silver sheen of stretching seeming peace which has no end of waters. Tourists, attracted by the history of Epe in the underneath of its scalding earth, come and depart again, leaving, as I have left only to return again. Round-onion-circled; again.

Again came on a Sunday, driving from Ibadan to Epe in a convoy of cars; Black Diasporans breathing the air, anticipating the swimming in the Atlantic; the eats, the inevitable barter of goods, which, as we sat on the grass, the indigenes would bring to us, to sell.

And you could tell in the manner of his greeting that he was used to foreigners. He was an old man whose back heaved with the weight of age and the sack he carried over his shoulder. There were lumps in the sack. He sat down cross legged, rheumy eyed, and grinned a toothless grin. "I get something you never see before" he said amicably. He caressed the rounds in the sack.

And they were hard rounds. I could see that. That they were hard rounds.

"You haven't brought onions to show us have you? Ancient onion artefacts?"

He appeared bewildered. He reached for the end of a wrapper and wiped his face.

"It no be onion-oh!"

It was a lie. A gross deceit which would be uncovered and brought to light before the day was over and over. Onions were in that sack. There were hard rounds in it; large. And believing-seeing appetite in him for onion fare, I thrust, not so benignly thrust before him, my dish of onion rings, fried in batter. They lay flat on the plate in so many circles. He sniffed them, his nostrils twitching. He asked me what they were. Onion Rings. He wide opened his eyes. Surely they could not be onions? He would try one. Just to see how it tasted. He spat it out, his eyes now narrow with bitterness. I had deceived him into thinking that onions which grew in the earth were the same as those coated in batter and then fried in hot oil. I had crossed him.

He delves into the sack. There is a bang and a clink of iron. He does not remove whatever is inside. He is a master of suspense and he grins his toothless grin; much is forgotten in the business of the day. He relates a history lesson of himself and of his Epe. The village used to be a very important place in Nigeria. From Epe slaves were transported across the Atlantic to "other land" he said. In the olden days, he said; and he said he himself was a descendant of a Chief who sold 'difficult' slaves 'across the water'. And I am certain, onion-remembering-certain, with every member of my Diasporan self, of onions in his sack; that I was one of those difficult slaves sold across the water.

He waits for this information to sink in; into the earth of my mind, and I try to stem longing for a slice of bread to place between my lips to prevent the hurt of my eyes which are filling with tears. He does not see them. The tears. He is unravelling the length of seeming innocence shining metal.

"This be Epe onion ring," he declares, his voice high as an Atlantic wave, his legs still crossed. The chains, slave chains, are passed from Black Diasporan hand to Black Diasporan hand by my companions who had listened to and watched this other encounter with chains. The old man's hands are still; like the Atlantic water, still. Still. My Black Diasporan hands refuse to touch the manacles. I believe that if I touch them they will cut-cut me. That the many layers of past life will be peel-peeled from me leaving me raw.

The slave chains have been wrenched from under an earth which was once my earth, grounding me before Atlantic crossing and divide; over sheen shine seemingly innocent waves, obscuring life-line; mine. Layered generations of black skin upon layered generations of black skin cut-severed and peeled, has not left me without eyes, mouth, ears.

And I ask the old man onion questions. Why are onion rings not included in African cuisine? Bold, upfront, upon a plate. Unhidden? He tells me he does not understand my question. I ask him to look at me carefully.

He stares.

"Do I have eyes, a nose, a mouth and ears?"

He shifts his position still cross-legged as he is; on the

grass; and enquires the reason for my seriousness. And why do I ask so many questions? Why are the *oyinbo du dus*, the *agerikes*, the *oyinbo* blacks, the descendants of slaves watching him in the way they are watching him? He was only doing a little business, a little trade in African artefacts and he did not usually "give his customers a history lesson."

He should charge us extra for that alone. The lesson as well as the cost of the slave chains. And then on top of that the *oyinbo du du* lady made him eat something which she knew he would hate. An onion ring.

I tell him I have one more question to ask. Just one; asking many. And I feel as if I have in my possession, though unseen, invisible, a huge sack which I have carried on my back for generations and am opening, reaching down into the sack, retrieving its contents and bringing it up to the light; and he sighs.

I ask him: "When you slice onions and put them in a pot with other things like oil and tomatoes --do you ever consider what happens to the onions, where they go to? What becomes of them? Do you still taste the onions and if you do, do you spit them out? Because I do. I do taste the onions even when they are coated in batter."

The old man studies my face.

"I true sorry. *Ma bi nu- oh!*"

No bread precautions threading my lips, my own sack emptied before his eyes I advise. I tell him that the next time he digs in his yard for slave chains he should not on any account try to sell them to *oyinbo du dus*, Black Diasporans. He should...

"I true sorry. *Ma bi nu-oh!*" he repeats. Next time, when we come to Epe, he consoles, he will bring us "better slave chains." He is so very sorry that the young lady is so obviously distressed just because he did not eat her onion rings.

The Good Woman/The Bad Woman

It was obvious. Their 'son' had married a bad woman who wanted her husband to herself. She would influence him; turn him against his 'real' family; the aunts and uncles, cousins, nephews and nieces and their daughters and their sons; in short his entire family clan. His wife was a bad woman. Selfish; that's what she was; she didn't want to share her husband with anybody.

If she was a white woman then it wouldn't be so bad. White people did not care about their families; let alone their extended one. But she was a Nigerian; his wife was a *tokunbo* girl of course, born and educated in England, and nothing good came from that quarter. Just wait. She would alienate him, her husband, their son, from the whole family. Then where would they go? What would become of them? They wouldn't be able to stay and live in his house as was their right; family right. They wouldn't be able to get a little cash or a gift from him. She, his wife, would take everything for herself.

His wife had served the first course and the second. Then she asked her husband, their very own son, in whose veins ran their very own blood to make them coffee and serve them ice-cream. That was why she, as his old aunt, the eldest in the family had had to put her foot down. She had had to put both feet down and demand that his wife serve them. What was she thinking of asking them to serve themselves? At least his

Tokunbo wife had had the sense to comply. But she was simply biding her time, bad woman that she was, waiting to send them away. These *tokunbo* girls were too selfish. They just couldn't be trusted. They were out and out bad women.

"Eh heh! You see my son," she began.

She was his aunt-in-law on his father's mother's cousin side of the family.

"She done listen to everything we dey talk. She is dangerous oh!"

And she walked in. The *tokunbo* wife.

"Good morning auntie."

The greeting, though specific, was addressed to the gathering, and her husband, who sat in the midst of what she saw as a substantial part of his village, was squeezed in on this side and on that.

Strewn around the room and particularly near the main entrance of the house were bundles and an assortment of boxes and suit-cases -- the luggage of the clan which they had brought with them only the night before. She heaved a sigh of relief. Thank God they had decided to spend only the one night instead of the proposed month or so; a thought which had frozen her to the marrow. It wasn't that she didn't want them to come and stay—but not a whole village and certainly for not such a long period as they had seemed to want to remain in the house – at least as evidenced by their luggage. Besides they hadn't enough room to accommodate his family. And how were his relatives going to be fed? At the rate at which they consumed the pounded yam and *egusi* soup and ice cream, she and her husband would be broke in a couple of days. And what would his family be doing in Lagos and in their house while she and her husband went out to work? Thank God his relatives had decided to leave.

The aunt frowned. The other relatives, her husband hemmed in by them, stared at her unabashed; malevolence in the very way their elbows hugged the sides of their bodies and their feet clung to the flooring. She counted them mentally. Fifteen. Thank God they had assessed her as the *tokunbo* girl who was so westernized and educated that she cared nothing for her husband's extended family; was selfish and wanted her husband all to herself. She was a bad woman. Thank God they thought she was a bad woman. Now they would return to the village.

"Auntie, you've obviously decided to leave us. So soon? It's a pity you can't stay longer."

"Eh-heh! You fit sorry?" demanded the aunt, the other relatives listening to the altercation with avid interest.

Perhaps she had already said too much. But this Aunt had decided to leave, thank heavens. And the family's luggage packed and the bundles placed next to the door could only mean that they were on their way back to the village.

She wasn't prepared for what happened next.

The aunt, a comfortably large woman dressed in her best George wrapper with an elaborate blouse with lampshade sleeves dotted with a multitude of artificial pearls, paying no heed to her dress, promptly threw herself on to the floor and rolled over and over from one side of the room to the other with an agility which was truly amazing for one so huge. As if on queue the relatives raised their hands above their heads and a rising fully textured cacophony of soprano, tenor, and bass tones instantly filled the room; voluminous in depth, a kind of musical accompaniment to the rolling figure of the aunt. Her *gele* even had the sense to detach itself from her head. The aunt paused for breath and crawling forwards replaced the *gele* tucking in the more stubborn flaps. This action being effected the aunt began to shout.

"Ah! to think-oh! I can't believe it! I beg, bring me water! No! Bring gin. Gordon's – I see-am inside drink-box cabinet. And bring...wetin' ?..bring iced-cream. Make I cool down."

She quaffed the gin neat, and after finishing a bowl of ice-cream, admonished the relatives.

"Be quiet-oh!" Her *gele* in place, she spoke: "You say we must leave our son's house!

This be terrible day-oh!"

With that she began a convulsive sobbing and the relatives knelt around her, some petting her with soft voices; some attempting to wipe her tears which bore a curious resemblance to the pearls on her blouse.

"Auntie I never said that you should leave our house. You're welcome to stay if you want, for as long as you want."

"Bless you my daughter, my wife. I know say that you be *tokunbo* girl but you never selfish. I see that for your face long time. I know you done pretend when you say you never want me   stay for your house...Your husband family. You good woman."

With the help of two cousins on his mother's sister's side the aunt was lifted to the chair and immediately began to instruct the others as to where to put this or that bag; this or that bundle; then she quit the room leaving the couple alone.

The speed with which the aunt had dealt her a blow, not a physical one of course, but a much more profound one, left her exhausted.

Her husband still sat on the settee.

"God alone knows how long they're going to stay," he said,

"And we simply have neither the space, nor the funds to feed them."

"Why didn't you say something? Tell that aunt of yours that we can't maintain a whole village in our flat. She would take it from you. I'm the bad woman, remember?"

"You're now the good woman, remember? What are we going to do? How are we going to cope? Did you see the way Auntie ate the ice-cream? That sweet tooth of hers is going to ruin us."

"No it won't. Do I have your permission to get auntie and the rest to leave? Husband, mine?"

"Sure. But if you can try and do it in . . ."

"A good way?'" she grinned. "I'll go get auntie right now."

She returned with a thoughtful-looking Auntie.

"Our wife is not necessary to talk more. *Wahala* don finish. I know sef you be good woman. That is why we fit stay three, four months with our son."

She tweaked her 'son's' cheek.

He grimaced.

"Auntie, I don't know how to say this, but we don't really have enough room for everyone," her husband began.

"My son, I cannot stay here alone-oh. It never matter. We can sleep for floor. *Shey bi* we are family, not so?"

Mentally she rolled before Auntie on the floor of her thoughts from this side to that side to an imagined rising cacophony tenor, bass, soprano.

"Auntie you know I love you. This is the first time I've been privileged to meet you and my husband's family. It's just marvellous to have you here."

"Bring me gin," demanded the aunt.

Her 'son' left to do the aunt's bidding.

"Eh heh. Now talk. You say 'privileged' and 'marvellous'. Big grammar you talk. You are good woman. Not selfish, our wife."

"Thank you Auntie. Actually . . ."

She sat beside the aunt.

"Actually Auntie, I believe I am a good woman as you say and I...um noticed your sweet-tooth."

"Eh-heh"

"And, Auntie I've planned all sorts of delicious meals for you, and...er the others"

"Others?"

"I mean Auntie, the family"

"Eh-heh"

"I've planned to cook the family...well...I've planned to cook you things I've picked up in England."

"The pounded yam and *egusi* soup it too sweet for last night."

"Why thank you, Auntie."

"What kind thing you go give us for food?" asked the aunt. "Where that boy with my gin?"

"I believe we've run out of gin and I'm afraid the yams, *amala* and the melon seeds—they're finished"

"Which kind thing you go cook for us?" repeated the aunt, sinking more into the cushions.

"There's . . . let's see . . . steak and kidney pie, leeks and mashed potatoes . . ."

The aunt removed her *gele* in a futile attempt to stuff its overlapping pieces into the crown.

"And Auntie because you have an obvious sweet tooth, I thought I'd make an assortment of English puddings for you like...let's see... 'frog's spawn' and then there's 'toad in the hole' . . . that's not a sweet dish of course but . . ."

"Toad?"

"They are like frogs but it's actually sausages in a kind of pancake batter and…"

Auntie whistled, and as if the relatives had been awaiting this signal, they emerged one by one. At least two or three had already become accustomed to the beds in the house and had to be awakened from sleep.

"Where my son?"

"He's probably gone somewhere to find the gin," said the *tokunbo* wife amicably.

"Eh-heh"

The relatives were told by the aunt to repack their luggage. They were leaving for the village that very hour, that very day.

"When my 'son' come, tell-am say the *palava* for dis house too much."

"I don't think I follow."

The aunt, her *gele* in place, her voice loaded with respectful venom asked, "You good woman, not so?"

"Yes Auntie I believe I am a good woman."

"Is true. You good woman. Tell my 'son' I no fit stay in your house. Tell-am say his wife too good for Auntie."

Too good for Auntie. Too bad for Auntie, she reflected.

And when her husband returned and listened to what had transpired between his aunt and his wife, she poured him a not so obvious glass of good bad good gin.

Bitter Leafing Woman: Part One

Blessed above women shall Jael the wife of the Heber the Kenite be; blessed shall she be above women in the tent.

He asked water, and she gave him milk; she brought forth butter on a lordly dish.

She put her hand to the nail; and her right hand to the workman's hammer; and with the hammer she smote Sisera, she smote off his head, when she had pierced and stricken through his temples.

At her feet he bowed, he fell, he lay down; at her feet he bowed, he fell. Where he bowed, there he fell down dead.

Judges 5:24-27.

Forty years, she thinks; forty years long Satan-standing; standing years . . . and she a cook; his Christian cook has been living in a forest of wilderness bitter leafed for forty years.

Forty years, the ultimatum given to her by her master, her fiancé of forty years, a Deacon of the Church.

The Deacon has said that it will take forty years to groom her into his wife; a suitable Christian wife. And the forty years of grooming have ended; and she thinks, bitter leafing thinks, of those past forty years; turning over in the pages of her mind; as she has turned over and over again the pages of her Bible; the pages of Deacon's ultimatum: "My dear in order to be a suitable wife to a Deacon of the Church you must read your Bible every day and when you learn how to be a wife of a man of God I will marry you in forty years time."

That was the genesis of it all. The Eve and the evening when he said those words; and she begins with Genesis and she sees Eve in a beautiful garden of Eden; she sees Eve plucking a forbidden fruit and giving the fruit to her husband Adam; and Adam eating; and then the banishment because of Eve's deception and woman willingness to be deceived; and the banishment into a forest of bitter leaves which churn and turn and churn in her with bitterness; leaved.

In this kitchen of the Deacons' mansion where she prepares the bitter leaf for him which he so much likes, she thinks of Eve before the fall naked and unashamed; she thinks of the clothing which came after the fall and how Deacon is clothed, his man's legs clothed in trouser lengths; which enter his voice when he says that she should not; not dress in the garb of men; should she do thus she would become a man like him in wanting to be a man and lord it over him with female deceitful female wanting.

And she threw the lengths of trousered - only for male meant-away. She had thrown male clothing away.

And he ate the bitter leaf soup she had prepared. He ate it and licked his lips.

She had, though not yet been wived; servant-obeyed her trouser wearing master when he said, Deacon said: wives be obedient to them who are your masters as unto Christ. She had servant-obeyed him.

And he ate the bitter leaf soup she had prepared. He ate it and licked his lips.

She had obeyed him when told of Jezebel made up Jezebel: A would be Christian wife does not Jezebel herself into marriage by wearing makeup; and making up that which God Himself has made.

You are lovely the way you are. A simple Christian cook un-made up.

And her makeup making up she threw her makeup away.

And he ate the bitter leaf soup she had prepared. He ate it and licked his lips.

Even when she told him, said-told him of that made up trousered woman he brought and bedded in this very house her bitter leafed heart churning . . . even . . .

Be silent woman he said. Be silent.

And she was silent unspeaking of bitterness.

And he ate the bitter leaf soup she had prepared. He ate it and licked his lips.

His hard hand striking her mouth to ensure silence; he ate the bitter leaf soup she had prepared. He ate it and licked his lips.

And now tonight the years of bitter leaf engagement have ended; have come here and now in this kitchen; and she has judged and she has been judged and she has been reading the Book of Judges, its pages bitter leafed.

Deacon is here. Deacon says he knows forty years have ended but he cannot marry her. She has been expecting his words.

And...she has...and she has tried not to judge him.

Touch not my anointed and do my deacon prophets no harm.

She has tried not to judge him; to harm him.

Her mind churning bitter-leafed she has tried not to judge him; to harm him.

No harm…for the men in the bitter leafed Book of Judges when she met the made up woman cut-sliced- up into twelve pieces; her woman's body sent back and back on her back to the twelve-fortyed tribes of Israel. No harm done to them. No harm.

And she looks around this kitchen-room; sees judging from the Book of Judges Jael a hammer in her hand; and Jael hands her the hammer; leaves the kitchen and leaves her bitter – leaved; the hammer in her hand.

The tent of Jael is her kitchen. Jael judged heroine for murder of Sisera and Deacon is Sisera.

Sisera and Deacon want bitter leaf soup.

And she goes to the stove where the bitter leaf soup has been simmering for forty years; but she turns as only a woman can turn removing her dress; tearing it into long strips; her woman's body naked and unashamed.

And Deacon watches her bemused; he wants to eat the bitter leaf soup she has prepared. He wants to eat it and lick his lips.

He wants to . . .

She says she will serve him the bitter leaf soup on a lordly dish and his eyes grow soft with a longing and desire he has not felt for her for forty years; the longing and desire has been given to other women to satisfy his appetite for this long waiting for his marriage to her.

And he casts a glance at the bitter leaf soup and he licks his lips. His eyes large with wondering at his Christian woman cook who has stripped herself naked and bare.

He forgets the bitter leafing cooking Christian cook woman before him when he sees the hammer in her hand.

Deacon forgets to lick his lips when he sees the hammer in her hand.

His hands stretched out in blessing Deacon says he forgives her; forgives her for her transgressions. He will marry her; tonight he will marry her.

And the hammer is in her hand and she looks at the hammer in her hand and thinks it the most beautiful hammer she has ever seen; it is a hammer which has been hammering her; in her, bitter leaved for forty years.

Deacon forgets the bitter leaf soup cooking on the stove and he forgets to lick his lips when he sees her looking at the hammer in her hands and Deacon says: Judge not lest ye be judged. Touch not my anointed and do my deacons no harm. Judge not.

And when he says 'judge' the hammer in her hand rises and she moves to the kitchen table where Deacon sits; his eyes amazed at the expression in her eyes, her normally obedient eyes.

With the hammer in her hand raised high
With the hammer in her hand raised high
She strikes Deacon's head
Forty bitter leafed year times
She strikes his head
Deacon falls from his chair at her feet
At her feet he falls from his chair
At her feet, at her feet, he moans
He moans at her feet.

And she binds his bloodied head with the strips of her clothing

She binds up the wounds of his head

He is alarmed he says; he is alarmed that she a Christian cook should have behaved in a manner so un-Christian; but, he says he forgives her for her ungodly act.

He will marry her as soon as she repents of her dastardly deed

Why? She could have killed him!

He wants to eat the bitter leaf soup she has prepared.

He wants to eat the bitter leaf soup she has prepared and lick his lips.

He says she needs penance. It will take forty years for her to repent of her sins and this great sin of attempted murder.

And she says: At my feet Deacon bows.

At my feet Deacon fell and Deacon lies down;

Deacon lies down. He lies down. Down.

At my feet Deacon lies down dead.

To me Deacon is dead.

And bitter-leaf-left.

Deacon is bitter leafing-left.

Bitter Leafing Woman: Part Two

The Workman's Hammer

Blessed above women shall Jael the wife of the Heber the Kenite be; blessed shall she be above women in the tent.

He asked water, and she gave him milk; she brought forth butter on a lordly dish.

She put her hand to the nail; and her right hand to the workman's hammer; and with the hammer she smote Sisera, she smote off his head, when she had pierced and stricken through his temples.

At her feet he bowed, he fell, he lay down; at her feet he bowed, he fell. Where he bowed, there he fell down dead.

Judges 5:24-27.

It was the nature of the crime, rather than the crime itself which stupefied, which baffled many.

Particularly Nigerian men.

First she served him bitter leaf soup in a lordly dish. Then she picked up the hammer which she used to smash the heads of coconuts and smashed-banged his head with that very hammer. His surprised body sagged to the floor. His wounded eyes stared at the bitter leaf soup in the dish which was a lordly dish.

It was in all the Lagos dailies. Was she mad? Are women in general mad? Why did she trouble herself like that? Serving him bitter leaf soup in a lordly dish like the newspapers said, even, it was rumoured, going so far as to recite a verse of scripture from the Bible, and then bash him on the head? Was she menopausal? Was it her time of the month? Would Deacon, her fiancé of forty years standing, survive the blow or blows? Did she in fact serve him, along with the bitter leafing soup, a single blow or several blows of severance with the hammer she used for splitting the heads of coconuts?

And that was another thing . . . Did she really mean to kill him in such a brutal manner? There were guns and knives a-plenty in Lagos. But her choice of weapon was a hammer. Her poor fiancé . . .he was lodged in the Emergency Section of General Hospital, his head bandaged in cloths which she had already torn into thin cotton strips, the remnants of her night-gown some said . . .before the attempted murder.

Given the type of crime with its food-woman dimensions, I wasn't too surprised when MID, Male Investigating Detective, rang my doorbell. I was in my nightgown and about to go to bed, but I ushered him into the kitchen, the room where I can think things out, where I create recipes, where I cook and where I eat; and where I serve the food which I cook or do not cook. It is the room where I dream dreams of marination.

"Have a seat. Make yourself comfortable," I told him. "I was just about to have a light supper before going to bed . . . bitter leaf . . ."

His face blanched as I brought the bitter leaf soup dish to the table, taking care to ensure it was a lordly dish.

"I'm so sorry for intruding like this . . . oh! No, thank you, nothing for me. This is strictly a business visit. It's . . . it's a matter of great urgency," he said with that male directness, thrust, which I had grown accustomed to in my crime-female-food investigations all over the world.

I stared at the dish of bitter leaf soup and he watched me and the bitter leaf soup and the dish and he said, "You must have heard of the terrible crime."

I nodded.

"I don't know what's come over you women. It's not only that crime, but women . . . Oh I don't know . . . It's overwhelming!! It's just flabbergasting!"

He leaned the bulk of his body forward, his eyes outward-scanning, his voice a low, hoarse and very masculine whisper.

"I've come to ask for your assistance on the case."

"At night? And why may I ask did you think it necessary to bring a hammer along with you?"

For I had suddenly noticed a hammer which he had placed on the table. With all that I had heard about the attempted murder and the role of the hammer in that scenario the sight of it was not a little disconcerting.

"At night . . . yes, don't be alarmed by that hammer. I do some carpentry odd jobs for people in the neighbourhood in the evenings. I shouldn't have brought it . . . what about the case?"

Again I stared at the dish of bitter leaf soup between us on the table. Then I smiled for him a ready smile, a helping smile and a serving smile.

"You mean, I suppose, the case of the woman who attempted to murder her fiancé with the hammer she normally used to bash the heads of coconuts?"

"Umm...yes," he faltered, his eyes again traversing the corners of my kitchen. "You women are sometimes painfully explicit," he murmured, pulling his body back from the table with some effort.

He was dressed in plain clothes as they say . . . a tee shirt of tie- dye blues and browns, jeans and sandals. He had dark, mahogany- textured skin. His eyes were almond shaped with long sweeping eyelashes upturned, which, when he lowered them, gave him a coy feminine look which skipped his aquiline nose, disregarded his high cheek bones and struck up a relationship with a full sensuous mouth, which . . . strange for a man of his bulk and height . . . quivered when he spoke.

"Madam, I . . . we at the police force want you on this case. We're rather desperate. In fact it wouldn't be an exaggeration to say that practically every adult male in Nigeria fears for his safety. There's been such a spate of violence, brutality meted out by women to their men-folk throughout the country . . . this recent attempt at murder . . . and I hear the woman had the audacity to cite a scriptural murder to justify her action . . . I...I don't know what's gotten into our women."

"Our women?"

And my smile is a soft hardness.

"I'm sorry, forgive me. Why, we at police headquarters . . . name it, Lagos, Jos, Kaduna, Enugu, Ibadan . . . north, south, east, west . . ."

"I am aware of the points of the compass . . ."

"Madam, we've been inundated by requests from husbands, uncles, sons, nephews and fathers-in-law and fathers and even a few grandfathers . . . that we should increase surveillance on their . . . I mean on women. It's . . . we're at our wits end. It's costing us a lot of manpower."

Manpower.

I let that one pass.

So the adult male population of Nigeria were at their wits end . . .

"It's as if our, I mean, the women have suddenly become hostile to us men. I can't think why . . . but it's downright scary."

"You're afraid of women?"

The question made him drop his eyes and their eyelashes formed a light, almost imperceptible, shadow on his face. I helped him out by re-stating the original cause of his concern and the reason behind his visit.

"And the culmination of this spate of purported female aggression has to do with, or lies in the woman who served her fiancé bitter leaf soup on a lordly dish, then picked up a hammer . . . a hammer like the one you've brought . . ."

And on impulse I grab the hammer and put it on the floor. I don't know this man. He might be a detective but when's all said and mostly done he's a man.

And we're both looking at the bitter leaf soup and at the hammer until he breaks the silence and says he believes I am the one to solve the case; I am the one to interview the Christian cook who attempted to murder her Deacon fiancé of forty years. He says, "You are the man for the job."

Man for the job.

I let that one pass too.

He was a nice enough fellow, eyelashes and mouth especially.

"I hope you're not just sweet-talking me."

"Madam we're desperate. This female thing with murder in the eyes of our females, our women, for us men, why . . .

Will you help us?" he asked, and when I answered in the affirmative, he brightened up considerably and he grinned, his face boyish.

"Madam, WFD, do pardon me, but you are extremely strange, the strangest of your sex, your gender I have ever come across . . ."

He's leaning forward across the table, leaning forward over the lordly dish of bitter leaf soup . . . It seems my strangeness is a magnet drawing him close.

"I can tell that you're somewhat apprehensive about me, MID. Perhaps I should put this bitter leaf soup away?"

MID shuddered. "I wonder if we men will ever understand you women. But thank you for agreeing to help on the case. I think I'll take my leave now. Please kindly let me know when you're done. What's your real name by the way? I know that you are a kind of detective and that you call yourself WFD or Woman Food Detective, but what's your real name Madam?"

"What's your real name MID?"

He smiled and looked deep into my eyes and I confess I felt the very slightest of tremors when he did that. I had never fallen in love with anyone before; never felt the way I was feeling with this MID chap before. Falling in love wasn't part of my business and with this particular crime before me I wasn't about to be derailed by the enemy.

To remind myself of the business in hand I spooned some bitter leafing soup in my mouth. And I told him to give me some time and I would get back to him after I had completed my investigations.

He had taken the first bite of my story. And the very morning after I met him I got busy with my investigations; talking to the various dimensions of the crime; the Emergency

Section of General Hospital; the hammer which was used to smash the heads of coconuts but was used instead to hammer the head of my clients' fiancé Deacon; bitter leafing soup, and of course my client herself; the woman who attempted the murder of her fiancé.

That MID man is so very handsome . . . those eyelashes . . . but I must continue with my investigations . . . that MID man is really, really handsome . . .

****

It's been forty years since I've been on this case and I have been seeing MID for forty years day in and day out. It's the first time in my life that I have taken so long to handle a case and I confess I have rather drawn things out. I have been marinating in MID's presence; and though I have contacted the woman whose fiancé the Deacon had brutalized for forty years—the bitter leaf in the bitter leaf soup were most strident in their condemnation and bitterness about their role in the whole affair--thankfully the couple are still together and will be married under forty years.

Yes thankfully. I have interviewed them, the Deacon and his wife and indeed Jael, the hammer, and all those who participated in the murder...but most of all it is the hammer, the murder weapon I have to thank for illuminating my investigations . . .

Oh! MID is here in my Lagos kitchen as usual and he not as usual is spruced up and dressed in the most delicious *agbada* you ever saw. It hangs from his square shoulders and he adjusts its folds as he takes his seat in my kitchen. He asks me if we could move to the living-room so that we could be more comfortable and I agree. I have promised him that I will give him a fulsome report of the motivations behind the attempted murder this very day.

I agree and we leave my kitchen and enter the living-room. I do not ask him why he chooses that we should have our discussion in this living- room. I do not ask him why he has brought a busload of men who at this moment are waiting in my house, their hands clenching hammers.

For some reason I am anxious today . . . and I look at MID who is looking around my living-room; it is small and compact and beautifully decorated to my taste. On the walls are paintings, reproductions of food in various guises; there's Dali's 'Lobster Telephone' ; a huge photograph of bitter-leaf soup in a lordly dish of course; an interesting Japanese print of a geisha woman eating watermelon in a furtive manner on her knees in hiding, a Nigerian painting of a woman selling fruit in a market . . . the paintings are not decorations of course . . . they are to remind me of my business as WFD; the bookshelves are filled with certain cook books and the cook books contain recipes ;some male but mostly female recipes. In my line of work one has to be focused in case, just in case the other tries to derail you . . . cook up something behind your back and make you eat or engender gendered indigestible prejudicial foods . . . their own recipes, made up . . .

MID has never entered my living-room before and he gazes round without comment and on his face is a smile, a trifle enigmatic but still a smile; and he's smiling with those beautiful lips and his downturned lisping coy eyelashes are making the most sensitive shadows on his mahogany face.

Would that this moment could last forever; just the two of us in this living- room without any friction or thoughts of murder; or even of food, of things being cooked up, of bitterness ; just the two of us right here . . .

On impulse I go to my bedroom and change my dress. I can't be talking to him with him so dressed up and me in jeans and this old tee shirt. And I change into a dark green dress, the pleats like curved leaves; I still have to be focused about this murder and tell MID my findings.

When he sees me he gasps and he says I look beautiful but of course I am not going to fall for that sweet talking buttering the female up drivel thing.

"Well WFD, it's been forty years . . . what about the report you promised?"

And I get down to business and decide to tell him what Hammer, the murder weapon used by the then Deacon's fiancé to . . .

But he isn't listening. He says he's been coming to see me for forty years and then he says, "I do", he says staring at me earnestly. He says, "I do".

But feeling my face go hot and my hands clammy which is very unusual for a focused person like me I ignore his "I do" and continue speaking.

I tell him what Hammer told me of the hammering year after year for forty years . . . of how though he was a workman's hammer, a male hammer he felt so very bitter about the way Deacon struck his Christian cook friend and that was why he decided to align himself with the Christian cook's hand and bash Deacon's head; and besides his hammering was scriptural and besides one of his hammer ancestors was Jael's hammer and besides like his friend the Christian cook he felt bitter and bitter leaved . . .

MID doesn't seem to be listening to a word I've said and

he's moving closer . . . he wants to kiss me and I confess, over the past forty years I have been wanting to kiss him. He pulls back.

"Tell me your name, won't you? My name is Segun and it means as you probably know- victory."

"Victory over what?" I ask.

"Why," he says, "Victory over myself. That's the only victory which counts isn't it? What's your name WFD?"

"It's Mojoyin if you must know."

"Mojoyin . . . honey. Honey," he says softly, "your name is honey. Under that hard exterior of yours I knew that . . . honey . . ."

I remind him that bees make honey but bees sting and he says "Yes, but they also make honey. They are known for it Mojoyin."

Just when I want to return to the subject of Hammer and throw in a thing or two on the sting of bees and not say anything about the honey they make so that Segun knows what's what; there is a knock on the door.

Segun in a somewhat lordly way which I discover I don't in the least bit object to, ambles towards the door and opens it for the busload of men with hammers in their hands . . . he says they have been waiting outside my house for forty years . . . how come I didn't see them?

But they've got hammers in their hands and my friend Hammer isn't among them...and I'm remembering murdering hammers and I'm remembering...bitter leafing woman thoughts crowd me . . .

But my fears are quickly allayed when Segun's smiling mouth announces that the men are his team of carpenters and the hammers they wield are working men hammers and the men and the hammers come from all over Nigeria.

"Lagos, Jos, Kaduna, Enugu, from the north, the south, the east, the west, the..."

I am told that they have been watching the developments and waiting for the resolution of this bitter leafing woman case for over forty years.

"Do you understand what is happening?" asks Segun.

I tell him "I do."

And I am saying I do and I do over and over again as I watch the carpenters use their hammers and their nails to expand my, our living- room. When they are done Segun tells me that if I don't mind they will come at various points over the centuries to include not only Nigeria but the whole world in our living- room.

But I'm not listening; not really. I'm not listening because Segun is kissing me and he is kissing me with the kisses of his beautiful mouth and his eyelashes touch my face and he's kissing me how he's kissing me. And my heart hammering hammers; my heart hammers in the most delicious way.

Sitting Policeman

Shola's heart beats; how it beats.

Ma Ronke with her ninety-eight year old nodding head and her hawk bright eyes and her gnarled crooked fingers will do her utmost best to spoil her engagement ceremony. Ma Ronke her eccentric great aunt is known for making life difficult; and when she acts in her role as Sitting Policeman she will use all of her pent up resentment against the youth . . . the youth are garbage to her . . . she will and has always used her age, her Sitting Policeman *ilopa ijoko* role to spoil things. Ma Ronke never smiles. Ma Ronke is a spoiler.

At the last engagement ceremony Ma Ronke used her role as Sitting Policeman and most revered eldest member of the family to slap her great granddaughter and why? Because she hadn't curtsied low enough in the old traditional way. And as if that wasn't enough; when Shola's own sister was beaming fit to kill that all had gone well at her own traditional engagement ceremony; and Ma Ronke hadn't done anything untoward; hadn't struck her mallet on the desk before her with force as she usually did; hadn't asked any embarrassing questions of the bride groom in her role as Sitting Policeman; just when it was all over and the families were about to party all day and all night with the newly engaged couple; Ma Ronke dropped her bomb.

It really was a bomb and it seemed to Shola that when that

bomb fell in the midst of the gathering every bit of happiness and joy were scattered. Her throat tugged and her heart beat so much she thought she would die right there.

Ma Ronke rose from her chair behind the desk; stooped to pick up her mallet of office and banged it hard on the desk. She scanned the room with those eagle eyes of hers and announced in her querulous vibrating voice, that she was, in a manner of speaking . . .

A manner of speaking?

Ma Ronke announced that she was going to die shortly. And looking in Shola's direction she said that she would probably die after Shola's traditional engagement ceremony; she hadn't quite decided, in a manner of speaking, whether she would die during the ceremony or directly afterwards. They would have to wait and see, especially Shola. She wasn't sure whether Shola had what it took to be married to a man like Pade. Ma Ronke said that she had talked to Shola and Pade; and what she knew about Pade was that Shola wasn't the kind of girl . . .

Girl?

Who could live together with her intended husband Pade as man and wife. Pade was intolerant. Shola was intolerant. They had to learn to bury their intolerance and make their love more alive than they thought it was.

Perhaps, in a manner of speaking, her death would teach Shola and Pade a lesson; an alive lesson.

Shola's face grew hot with embarrassment at that time; and with the others present she waited for the buzz of chatter which followed Ma Ronke's death announcement to die down.

And when it did, Ma Ronke, ignoring Shola's sister who was after all the one who was becoming engaged and should be the object of attention; Ma Ronke spoke to Shola and she said, "Shola in a manner of speaking you are a good girl but you do not, unlike your sister have what it takes to be a married woman. I shall say no more; but you will see the fruit of my words at your own engagement ceremony or perhaps afterwards in a manner of speaking . . . ."

In a manner of speaking . . . Ma Ronke was staring at her today, her engagement day and her heart beats increased so much she couldn't enjoy anything . . . the tent, the balloons and the decorations, the music as she sat in a throne like chair an empty one beside her waiting for Pade to sit like the chair sat beside her.

Ma Ronke . . . she had promised to die either during Sola's ceremony or directly afterwards.

Shola tries to blank out her fears. She tries to conjure up some joy at the sight of the crowd of women and men accompanying Pade into this huge tent; the carpeted floor jostling with fruit; the drumming music and the songs and the dancing feet and Pade . . . her Pade a huge smile on his face; the gifts which her fiancé Pade's family have brought for the ceremony . . .

She tries to focus on the sound of the drumming and the hands of the drummers as they beat into her heart the excitement of this day and of her marriage to Pade but she cannot; her mind is a convoluted mass of worry. Ma Ronke is going to spoil things, everything on her engagement day.

And to think that the old woman had sat her down and told her that she loved her so much; to think that she, Shola, had pleaded with her not to spoil her engagement day.

And now here in this other room, this fairy tale tent which

with her friends she has decorated the night before, Shola regards her great aunt. If Ma Ronke had planned to die today like she promised; she didn't look the least bit frail. She was grasping her mallet; glaring around the tent as if she was ready and preparing herself for the trouble which she would definitely cause. Just because Ma Ronke was old she thought that everyone would do her bidding without question. She was using her age as a licence to spoil everyone's life; especially her own Shola life.

The drummers, the men and women accompanying Pade have gone to their seats and in the silence Shola worries. Pade hasn't got a job. He hasn't been able to find any kind of employment even though he is a graduate; but she has a job; she has a job; she will take care of him and the baby when it comes; she has a job.

And when she looks at Pade, her love for him floods her like never before. Whatever Ma Ronke says or does . . . and even if she does die and even if she doesn't die . . . all will be well. This fairy tale tent and happily for ever after tent tells her so.

And Shola does not remember how and when the music and the joy stops. It suddenly stops. And Ma Ronke is sitting upright in her Sitting Policeman chair and Ma Ronke is beating on the desk with her mallet so fiercely that Pade turns around and faces Ma Ronke.

"Silence everyone!" she shouts and with her querulous voice Ma Ronke says that there will be no exchanging of love letters; no reading of love to the families of Shola and the family of Pade as is the custom. She wants to interview Pade in her role as Sitting Policeman and she wants to do so right now; at this very moment.

She was the Sitting Policeman wasn't she? She was the oldest person in both families wasn't she?

The tent waits and Ma Ronke again strikes her mallet on the desk so forcefully that Shola thinks the desk will be reduced to splinters the way Ma Ronke strikes it.

"What are you waiting for Pade?" Ma Ronke shrieks "Prostrate!"

Pade kneels on the floor.

"Is that the way you prostrate before your elders young man? The youth of today!"

Pade lies prone on the carpet. He presses one cheek to the floor. He presses his other cheek to the floor. He rises.

"Did I tell you that you can get up Pade?"

Pade lies down low on the carpet. And he is told to rise.

"Today is your traditional engagement ceremony Pade. And might I remind you that in our culture, the Yoruba culture, this ceremony is more important than a white wedding? Perhaps with all of your dancing you have forgotten! Pade do you love our daughter?"

"Yes, Ma Ronke I love Shola with all my heart. She is the sugar in my tea, she is the cream in my coffee, she is . . ."

"So Shola is the sugar in your tea? She is the cream in your coffee? You are more ignorant than I thought young man! The first question I ask you . . . I will repeat it again. And before you answer my question think carefully before you answer. Now Pade . . . the fruit of your union . . . if our family agrees . . . will depend on your answer. Don't be surprised if I ask you to leave this tent without your bride!"

And here Ma Ronke as was her habit paused for what seemed to Shola like a million years. And in those million years of thought she glanced at her family sitting in their purple and yellow *asoke* their white lace; she gazed at Pade's family in their olive green and orange *asoke* outfits specially made for this occasion. And she saw embarrassment written on every piece of clothing and on everyone present.

"Are you listening to me Pade?"

"I am listening Madam."

"Very well. Do you have a job Pade? Mr. Coffee and Mr. Tea?"

"Madam I have applied for several jobs but although I am a graduate of Economics I have not been able to get employment yet Madam."

In her chair Shola ducks her head. She feels tears of frustration welling in her eyes. After this engagement she will have nothing to do with Ma Ronke. She really has gone too far this time . . . embarrassing not only her but both families with her stupid Sitting Policeman questions and she's calling Pade Mr. Coffee and Mr. Tea!

"Young man Pade. I asked you if you have employment."

"No Madam."

"How will you be able to look after our daughter Shola if you have no employment? How will you be able to pay for the sugar in your tea and the cream in your coffee young man? "

Pade is stammering and Shola can see his limbs stiffen with anger. He doesn't take well to criticism of any kind and if he loses his temper today that will be the end . . . the very end of any kind of engagement or marriage for them. And his lack of employment has been a weight weighing him down for three years since he graduated.

"I, I, I ,I. . ."

"You stammering fool of a young man," shouts Ma Ronke. "When I die . . . maybe after this announcement . . . you and

Shola must visit my tomb after one month of marriage. You and Shola must come together and perhaps we'll have tea and sugar and coffee and cream."

Ma Ronke is not smiling.

"Furthermore . . . no I've changed my mind. After my death in a few minutes or so . . . I want you to take my Sitting Policeman chair to your new home. Is that clear Mr. Coffee or is it Mr. Tea Pade?"

Shola and Pade and the friends and families present are shocked so shocked with Ma Ronke's speechifying and directives; clearly Ma Ronke has lost it. She's mad . . . she's . . .

In the kafuffle which follows Shola is not sure when it happens. She hears Ma Ronke coughing and coughing. She sees Ma Ronke slump and she sees men and women of both families rushing to Ma Ronke; lifting her out of her Sitting Policeman's chair and she stands at the opening of the tent watching Ma Ronke placed at the back of a car; they are driving her to a hospital. Ma Ronke has had a heart attack. As she had predicted Ma Ronke has died during Shola's traditional engagement ceremony.

Shola remembers now the desperate rush to conclude the engagement ceremony, her tears; the fast drive to the hospital and watching the still form of Sitting Policeman, Ma Ronke, no longer sitting on her chair; no longer a policeman sitting; Ma Ronke in all her funeral finery is just a corpse. She is dead. And Shola wonders if she will ever recover from this death.

****

They have been married one miserable month. It must be the child growing within her which makes her irritable with this jobless man. Pade has refused to work in her father's firm;

refused a fat salary and Pade has said that he is a man and a man has his pride.

"Are you ready to visit Ma Ronke's tomb Pade? We did promise . . ."

"Ma Ronke never said that we should visit her tomb she..." And Pade peruses the bought for them carpet and the bought for them chairs and the bought for them curtains --all bought by his parents- in- law; and Pade surveys the room which she keeps so very clean and spotless and Pade says that she , his wife, Shola is an untidy woman.

"Ma Ronke . . ." Shola begins . . .

And neither knows, is certain, how and where the slap comes from. Pade is looking at his hands and Shola is touching her cheek, her eyes filled with tears. She doesn't know why she tells him as she touches her smarting face that he should have gotten a job by now. Her father has an opening in one of his firms but Pade is too proud and . . . we are expecting a baby and we cannot continue to rely on my parents Pade.

Again he doesn't know where the slap comes from and why her whimpering sounds infuriate him the more.

And Shola on the floor shields her eyes. Her Pade has beaten her. He has slapped her. The man who has fathered the child within her has slapped her . . . as if he is some kind of policeman and he is saying that she caused Ma Ronke's heart attack and she Shola is the one who has brought bad luck on their marriage and she is the one who has prevented him from getting a job. She and her stupid Sitting Policeman great aunt Ma Ronke has made him slap her; has prevented him from getting a job. Her great aunt has cast a spell on them and that is why they've had to burden themselves with that stupid Sitting Policeman chair . . .

"Why Shola, did you against my wishes, put that idiotic Sitting Policeman chair in this living room --against my wishes? You're a spoilt brat, that's what you are! You and your family think you can buy me just because I haven't got a job! In case you don't know I'm the man in this family! Get up from the floor and go get me something to drink! I don't want to hear a word from you and that's final!"

"Final is it? Well, Pade and Shola, I, Ma Ronke, Sitting Policeman am not final in a manner of speaking; not final."

Both Pade and Shola look in the direction from which the voice comes; it is the voice of Ma Ronke, querulous, vibrating; it is her voice and it is coming from her Sitting Policeman chair.

"Yes it's me. Oh! The youth of today and the youth of yesterday and the youth of tomorrow . . . when will you learn that patience and sticking together no matter what is what you need." When will you learn Shola that you must tolerate and be sensitive to each others' shortcomings . . . when will you learn Pade that you must tolerate and be sensitive to each others' shortcomings . . . when will you learn to love each other no matter what . . .when . . .cream and coffee and sugar and tea and . . ."

Neither are sure of how and at what time Ma Ronke entered their living-room and the living-room of their thoughts . . . both are sure of what they hear; and what they hear is the mallet of the Sitting Policeman splintering the desk of their torment into a million pieces even with the knowledge that Pade may never find a job . . .

"Can we see you just once Ma Ronke?" asks Shola.

"We ghosts are not allowed to materialize in the way you want us to in a manner of speaking" Ma Ronke says, "But just this once for you my beloved Shola. Just this once . . ."

When they see Ma Ronke sitting upright in her Sitting Policeman chair both gasp at how youthful she looks, how vibrant, how real, how ever present. It is the first time Shola has ever seen her great aunt smiling. And the smile is a loving you no matter what smile and old smile and a young smile which instructs and guards kind of Sitting Policeman smile which they see on Ma Ronke's aged and youthful and old and young face.

Shola feels joy in her heart which beats; which beats; and Pade finds himself prostrating before Sitting Policeman; prostrating his full length before her.

Broken Plate

The widowed women, wedded in sorrow, draw close together; widows together. Gathering on this tight night they shut out the fears and the doubts of their hearts and break a plate.

Such a simple thing, the breaking of a plate.

The plate is an earthenware plate. Plain and heavy and old. It has been used in the heyday of its plateness to serve meals to a husband now dead in the underground earth. And this plate is held up for widowed eyes to see and widows ears to hear and widows hearts to break again as they are broken, have been broken, as it is held up by a woman clad in customary dark in shapeless *buba*; on her head a grey scarf tied, as she drops the plate to the concrete floor.

Pieces of broken plate on the floor. The widows. The pieces. The broken plate. Some might say it is a prating plate, its sound, as it breaks—the idle chatter of women. The widows believe it is a talk-discussing plate.

Talk, Broken Plate, talk.

"When my husband passed away— "

"Go ahead, continue. Don't stop. The time for tears is over. Speak. Our meeting here will change things. We widows have gone through a lot—everywhere in every part of this our Nigeria—we have rights, after tonight we'll do something. We'll change things.

Speak."

"They shaved me. They shaved me with a broken bottle . . . not, not only my head." She removes her scarf, reveals the bald wound of her naked head, tissued in laceration.

"They did it here too. No! I want to show you what they did!"

Her wrapper falls to the floor. Her hands move downward-deft-urgent pulling at her clothes under. And though the widows have heard with their ears of this, this—the skin—where her pubic hair—a network of swelling sores.

"I'm grateful that you looked, saw it—I—"

She reties her cloth, her scarf; resumes her sitting position.

"I kept my eyes closed the whole time they did it. Afterwards they gave me the hair—my own hair—I put it in—I kept it—"

Shaven. Shaven to show respect for her dead husband.

Broken Plate speak: "Na wa for my people oh! I no fit speak big grammar I beg. Forgive me-oh! I nearly vomit wen my husband people dem come my house, take me go im village and wash my husband corpse im body, hand, leg—dem pour water, dem squeeze water from sponge and put for calabash and say make me drink-am. I say no. I no gree drink dead water. I go sick if I drink-am. Dey say if I no drink-am, I be witch. Dat I poison my husband and I go show dem say I no be witch. I tell dem say I no be witch-oh! I no kill my husband. How I fit kill my husband? I born-am eight pickin. How I go be witch? Dem say dem go trouble me except I drink dead water. And I too tire, I get nobody wey go help me-oh and I drink the water. I vomit. Dem say if I no be witch I no suppose to vomit the water. As dem dey talk one kind man say I no look like witch."

Which part of the country do you come from?

Broken Plate speak: "I didn't have to do anything so disgusting as—God! drinking the water which they used to wash your husband's corpse—but although my husband died several years ago I can still remember the day my in-laws came. It was a fight to the teeth I can tell you. We owned—my husband and I—we owned a business. We put into it not only money—we always had a joint account you see—we put in time, effort, energy. The business belonged to both of us you see. No sooner had the news been broken—of his death I mean, than—I call it his village—his relatives descended. They even chartered lorries. Would you believe it? Lorries! To cart away our belongings. I'd just come home after dealing with the funeral arrangements—and it was terrible. Loss upon loss. They took my TV, video, fridge, furniture, my husband's clothing, my jewellery—everything gone—the carpet too.

I took a taxi to their village and they were so brazen! They told me I only had those possessions because of the wealth of my husband's business and that in actual fact the property belonged to him and now that he was dead—and that I'd probably killed him anyway—they said that now that he was dead the property belonged to them—I can't tell you how angry, upset, I was. I was sort of floating between grief and shock. Those same in-laws who had stayed at our house for months on end and who I had no quarrel with did that to me—It was hell I can tell you!"

Are you Igbo, Itsekiri, Kanuri, Yoruba?

The widows look at the floor and at the broken pieces of the earthenware plate, scattered. It is scattered. It was once a circle wedded-tight, the plate. Now the plate is broken, its edges sharp.

"Thank God my husband made a will and insisted that we

sign both our names for the property. Some of my in-laws wanted to contest the will, but they gave up. If it hadn't been for that will I would be penniless today. Imagine…I used to feed these very people."

"Do you eat *amala* and *ewedu* in your part of the country or *ogbono* soup?"

Broken Plate Speak:

"I, I'm sorry, I, I, I, had to stay with the corpse in the death chamber. Yes, that was what it was, a death chamber. Everyone insisted I do it. They tied my leg to the bed. And then I had to stay there. It's a miracle to me today that I just didn't die. Two deaths. Two corpses. It was just me with the corpse in the room."

Her eyes dart at shadows flitting across the walls, disembodied eyes, as if awaiting the emergence of the ghosts of husbands dead.

"You, I recognize you—aren't you my, my late husband's sister? You were there when they forced me to sleep in the death chamber!"

"We have suffered, but it is our tradition. I've heard that some wives treat their in-laws badly and that's why they take it out on them when their husbands die."

Voices of Broken Plate speaking: "We must respect our culture."

"You know things like what happened to us happen in America and Europe."

"Being shaven isn't the horror you make it out to be."

Broken Plate speak: Another widow. She speaks of days and nights in a hut in the bush with only a fire, its flames licking her for an alive-warmth now dead; stoking the fire to keep her husband's spirit alive in widow vigil. Her dirty body unwashed, her uncombed hair uncombed until the night-walking ritual of cleansing bath in the forest dark, cleansing her from a dirt ritually agreed upon is hers; that is required; that is; is hers and hers only. And she speaks of the broken plate, dirty, from which she must eat and from which she must resist its beguiling sharp–edged edgedness which beckons 'Come cut your skin with me, break like I am broken. Take up this piece of my plateness and cut your vein in the throb where it pulsing throbs and join him, your husband in the grave. You are worthless; without the worth of your husband's life which gave you meaning. You are, if not dead, you are as dead. Dead.'cb

"I broke that plate at the beginning of the meeting—I broke it because, I wanted to show—"

Is your name Ngozi, Shade, Eriate, Hauwa? Which part of the country do you come from?

"I do hope no one gets to know of this meeting."

"They'll say we're disrespecting our culture."

"They'll say we're selfish and that we don't care about our husbands' spirits."

What tribe did you say you were from?

"I hope our husband's ghosts, our ancestors—won't come back to haunt us because of this meeting."

"I'm scared. I shouldn't have come."

"If we expose what we've gone through they'll say Africans are primitive."

"In Europe or America widows don't have a family support system like we do in Africa."

"And many of these customs are not applied today. Only in the rural areas and certainly no educated woman would put up with them."

"We mustn't give our culture a bad name."
"I broke that plate because I wanted to put an end to—"
"I must go home. I'll be missed. I'm sure I'll be missed."
Such a simple thing…the breaking of a plate.
"I feel better for talking about it, but—I must go home—"
Speak, Broken Plate, speak:
"I must go home. We—must—go—home. I. We—"

Dance of the Nursing Mother

Whiplash-falling-strike-hot-heated-falling; falling.
Falling on the beauty of his back.

His eyes trained on hers with an intensity which made the shuddering howl of her torment rent the air in an anguish of crying pain which she could not contain.

For the love of her he held high his head as the men lashed-struck his back; their reeling whips unfurled-flung against his male flesh of back; for the love of her, this rite of initiation. For the love of her this terrible in-held pain because he loved her; wanted to marry her; had . . . Had to show the whole village that he was the man he was and could bear pain; unflinching.

The village square was a red of two reds. The reddened natural colouring of the soil now deepened with the red of his blood. A tight band of onlookers pressed forward, cheering gesticulating, urging him to in-hold his breath, to be courageous-brave.

Another whip striking-whistling-in-the-air-about-him-on-him-whip and it would be over. He would have passed the test of his manhood, the Sharo, and shown the world of the village and himself; the self of him, that he was man and could marry his chosen bride, father babies, many children. He could withstand the pain of the whip without crying out and without shedding a single tear; the man in him.

His back was a criss-cross of lacerated weals, blood-encrusted; and still he held high his head, his eyes drinking from hers, a milky strength. He had always commented on the whiteness-pure of her eyes. They were like dark black coals set in a pool of milky white he had said. Was saying, silently saying aloud in his eyes, said; as the last strike of whiplash-falling-fell on his beautiful back and the jostling crowd, their necks strained, admiration on their faces, lunged forward, clapping, cheering, congratulating in an over-spilling of joy which danced over the pain of him; in him.

"You were..." tears streamed down her face, "You were so..."

He clasped her in his arms, his thoughts skipping lightly over their coming marriage and their child already within her and the coming birth which would make of him the proud father, man, that he already was.

He had passed the test. The Sharo test of manhood; and he had been further blessed. Among the other young men, only he had been able to get a much coveted job in Lagos. He had never been to the big city and when his childhood friend came to the village smelling of wealth, dressed in a suit and tie, driving the latest model of Mercedes with promises sticking close to his teeth; of more food than the village could eat in Lagos; for the taking – he had jumped like the whip had jumped on his back.

He too would go to Lagos and make his fortune. He had only to wait for the birth of his son – and the child would be a son, a man like him –and he had only to wait for his wife's own initiation; into motherhood; and then Lagos. Lagos . . .

"At least I won't be beaten with whips to show the world I'm a woman." She laughed into his thoughts. He rubbed her

170

stomach. "I don't want to frighten you but I've heard that labour pains are worse than any Sharo whip could be. You'd better not cry out!"

The whites of her eyes, milky as ever, gleamed back at him.

"I've learnt the steps of the dance" she said, "I will be the best dancing mother ever! I'll show the whole village, everyone, that I can . . . Do you want to see?"

"No. Not yet. You must be careful with the baby."

But when they arrived at her parents' hut she swirled around him in a graceful arabesque, her head dipping to a humming which entered the toes of her feet which touched the earthen floor and circled and lowered around him; her arms a cradling swoon of motion as she rocked the unborn child in a sway to the right and to the left of her and the humming became a crooning melody and he felt as if he was in a place so serene with a dreaming house of walls with her and with their baby . . .

"Be sure to dance like that when you dance the dance of the nursing mother."

He checked himself. The activity had aroused the child in untimely birth.

The night was long and he who had shown such courage when the whips lashed ran-rushed into the bush so that they, the women and his wife, would not hear the howling torment of pain in him.

Because he loved her. And because . . .

"He's lovely, yes. But are you alright?"

"Of course I am" she replied, putting the baby to her breast.

He regarded his son. "He's only a few hours old and he eats so much."

"He seems to love my milk," she murmured, gently pulling her husband down to the mat. He gazed at his son voraciously eating.

"How soon do you think you'll be strong enough to go to Lagos?"

"We can't go until he's about three months old. I want to get a job too in Lagos, and it would be better if I finish nursing him, breast feeding, before we go. Don't you think so?"

She saw the restlessness in him, the anxiety to leave the village, to begin his new job; his new life. *Theirs.*

"I, I don't want you to work. You are a woman; you must take care of our son. I am the one to work for the family and provide . . ."

"And then" she continued, wilfully ignoring his words "you'll have to stay for the dance . . ."

****

"I never said it was your fault."

"You might not say so but I know you're blaming me for...because we came to Lagos; you're blaming me because my friend tricked me, because I haven't got a job and you have one."

He turned away, backing her so that she saw his back.

"You're blaming me for everything. I can see it in your eyes."

"You'll awaken the baby if you don't keep your voice down."

The baby stirred in sleep.

"I'm doing all I can to help you until you can find a job. I'm buying the food ..."

The baby in his cot wailed.

She left him. She left them. She banged the door shut and walked the few yards to the main road to catch a *danfo*. It wasn't as if she wasn't doing her best to . . . since their move to Lagos he complained about everything and when she tried to reason with him . . . Recently he had even taken to locking himself up in the bathroom when the baby cried. Today an end had to be put to this incessant distress. She would stand up to him or leave. Whip, emotionally whip him into the Sharo-beaten-man-for-love-of-her she knew he was. It would mean perhaps losing a day's pay, but she was in no mood for work.

"Today, today," she said as she clambered down the steps of the *danfo* and crossed to the other side of the road to catch another bus. She would miss a day's work and return. Home. The night before she had told him of the rising cost of baby food.

Before their very eyes the child was losing weight. His reaction did not surprise her really. He did not quarrel. He did not speak. He had locked himself in the bathroom. She wasn't sure but the angry din which came from that quarter was . . . Oh! How I wish we would just go back to the village. Lagos . . . that wretched friend of his who said that Lagos was . . . who promised him a job . . . and then . . .

Rapidly she made her way to the flat. A flat only in name. It was more like a cave for animals than a habitation for human beings. The open sewers around it. The rubbish. The rats. The cockroaches. She had been able to persuade the landlord to give them another month's stay rent-free. After that . . . If she hadn't been lucky enough to get her job they would be out on the streets. Baby and all. Whether they could afford to buy Baby Food or not.

The door was open. Strange. "I'm sure I locked it."

She glanced quickly to the corner of the room to ascertain that the baby was there. The baby was nowhere to be seen. She called out her husband's name. With a sinking heart, a fear suddenly coming up upon her she screamed for her husband. Where could he have gone? He had long abandoned his search for work. Could he have gone out without locking the door? Without making sure that the baby was safe? And where was the child? She sat down, her head throbbing. Where was he?

Then it was that she heard a wailing; as if, muffled. It was coming from the bathroom. She ran, her hands flying, lashing out like raw flagellating whips against the door, and saw her husband; his body a doubled-over-hurting-pain. His head low, his mouth stuffed with cloth, his body heaving with the sobs which began their running-run inside her.

"The baby . . . where is the baby?"

She hadn't seen the child a gentle sleeping on the floor.

And she sat beside her husband and she rocked him gently swaying his body from side to side and he looked into the beauty of her milky white eyes and he asked her to dance the dance of the nursing mother because he had left Lagos for a job and a new life without her and had not waited for this dance.

And as she danced, her body in motion remembered the lash of the whip for her; the sting as it unfurled its long coil of length in a striking-blow-hit for the love of her in Sharo-

174

initiation-Sharo.

The blood of two reds and the awful spattering-spill of it on her heart; and she danced and she danced in an arabesque of swirling furl-twirl even as she danced.

And when he rose, his mouth empty of its choking cloth he clasped her and asked her to hold him hard in a wrapping embrace; so that the unhealed weals on his beautiful back hurt and he felt again his Sharo pain again with brave face looking at her, holding her apart, before he drew her to him, again.

Looking.

Looking at the white-milky-white-whiteness of her eyes which were her eyes.

Drinking;

And as he drank; of her milky white eyes, he entered the dance; the dance of the nursing mother.

Ice Cream Green

She knows with an inner certainty what will come on this day; first the venom spewed from an angry husband's mouth; his. Then will come the directive for her to leave the house and find another lodging; not his.

As she sits in this bedroom with its pale green walls; a green so innocent it makes her heart ache with unfathomable joy this green . . . as she sits in this bedroom she tells herself that she is prepared and has been prepared for this day; and she turns her gaze to the pale green walls; she wants to lick their greenness and get that green inside of her in a life; a life of green which must grow green in her heart. She wants the green inside this room to speak to her; and to grow green inside her. The green is ice cream green; and she remembers the first time she saw and she tasted green ice cream . . . so strange to see and taste an ice cream which was green . . . pistachio nuts grounded to dust to ashes dust but living still in another green . . . another ice cream green; and she remembers licking its melting greenness. On this day; the day of departure when she will leave her husband's house; she yearns for green ice cream. This is what she wants.

She wants to leave with her baby son, and, a catch in her throat, she looks at him, her baby son sleeping beside her. His bloated oversized head rests on the white sheets and his tongue a red distended thing juts out like a little bit of rubber jutting out; and she makes a promise to him. "I'll give you ice cream when you grow up" she whispers, "I'll give you green ice cream. Both of us will eat it. Do you hear me my darling son?"

They said that he would not grow up; he would not grow up. He would always be the way he was; deformed they said; deformed her husband said. He would never be like other children. "I'll give you ice cream when you grow up" she whispers again. And the baby's body is a body; a thing unmoving; his head big head moving; that bit of red tube jutting out; his tongue jutting out . . . She wants him so much to move really move; to understand that no matter what she will always be with him. In the days and the months and the years which will come when he will not respond to life, to her to no thing and nothing . . . this child with his big head . . . she has seen what such children become; vegetables they are called; better left in the dark underground earth to which they will go and which their life will be and will become. Better to terminate them. They are dead anyway. Wasn't that what her husband had said? But she had clung with a yearning hope that he would not be born vegetable like they said; her husband said; even after those tortuous nine long months of yearning months and the scans and the worried faces and the angry husband voice which said and said again :"He is better dead. The shame is too much. Get rid of him. He won't even know . . . Nigeria is not cut out to handle vegetables like that thing.

Simi for heaven's sake stop this nonsense. You've had the scan. Your son is a vegetable and will be a vegetable for the rest of his life. Get an abortion! Terminate the pregnancy!"

The angry venom spewed from the husband mouth. The slaps; and her resolution. She would have the child. And she had had the child and the child lay on the bed beside her.

The day had come; everything in the past three months had been building up to this day.

You have begged me for three months Simi. If he doesn't improve; if your son's head doesn't get smaller and shrink to the size of a normal child you will have to take him and leave. The both of you will have to go.

She knew then as she knows now that the child's head would never . . . The arguments of family and friends telling her that she should abort before it was too late; and even if it was. . . .

And since that time she has been distanced alone in a wanting green world and today . . . it is now that three month day of arrival and of departure. She has packed her things and she has packed his clothing and she is prepared. She lifts the baby on to her lap. His head droops and she puts him back on the bed. She might as well just tie him to her back but then his head . . . she will put him in a basket; much easier the basket. She has been gifted an apartment in Ikoyi . . . it is not really an apartment; it is one of the rooms in a friend's house. The friend comes and goes and doesn't really live in Nigeria. She has pity in her eyes for this mother of a deformed child and she has loaned the room to her. In exchange the mother will have to look after the house . . . and when the mother had looked at the room she felt so very grateful. This will be the room where her son will grow up; he will never be like other children; he will never be able to go to school; laugh and talk and play; his movements will be un-coordinated; his head will droop to one side. And worse still he will not know her or recognize her ever; but they will have this green room.

It's a great sacrifice you're making Simi. You've decided to break up your marriage and for what? He's not even a real human being. Can't you, can't I persuade you to get rid of this . . . aren't such children called mongoloid? Sorry to have to say that Simi but I just want you to face facts. You could easily have aborted him. It isn't a question of morality or anything. There were no surprises. You saw the scan and you had all the time in the world to change things. You're not being fair to him Simi. You're not being fair to him or your husband or to those who truly love you.

But the friend was a friend and had helped her. And over the past three months Simi has prepared that room and everything is ready.

Sitting here on this bed in this other room with its green walls around her she smiles; feels alive with the promise she has given herself and her baby son.

"That's what I'll do my darling son. Three months wasn't enough . . . when you're three years old; if you are alive and even if you're dead I'll open the tomb and give you green ice cream. I will put it in a glass and I will feed you with it and all will be well. Do you hear me?"

The baby, her son; her son with his big head lolling on the bed, his eyes bulbous . . . stares at her; and she says, "You must believe me. I know you can hear me. I'll feed you with a spoon and I'll see your eyes light up. We'll both wait for your third birthday!"

Her husband is in the room.

"Simi I'm sorry to have to do this," he says. "But even you must know that I can take only so much. I've ordered a car to take you and your son to your friend's house."

Simi is surprised at his calm voice. She had expected the venom to spew on this day; she hadn't expected him to be so matter of fact and so calm; so very calm.

And even now even she is surprised at the love she has for her husband.

She smiles and says, "We'll be alright."

He turns and quits the room.

He returns and says avoiding her eyes and the baby on the bed which he dares not look at and never has directly looked at since the child was born, "Simi, this is a great sacrifice you're making," he says. "And for nothing . . . for that . . ."

"It's not a sacrifice" she says picking up her baby. "Can't you look at him? Just once before we go?"

Her husband quits the room again and when she looks at its green pistachio ice cream walls she feels the green trembling inside her and she feels sobs enter her throat and the sobs sound green and the sobs are not for herself or her baby son.

Simi tells her baby son they are leaving this house. She promises her son that she will never leave him. She says "I will be with you always" and Simi leaves; she leaves.

She wonders why her baby cries in long wails which shriek and pierce her eardrums. Why he is attempting to swing his big head.

But Simi has been and is prepared. She covers her son with a small blanket. She whispers and croons to him. She rocks him backwards and forwards until the crying stops. She places her son in a basket and waits for the car to arrive; the car which will take them away to another room and another life ice cream green room life.

****

Life . . . she thinks as she sits in another life in another room and another room of life. Her son has been given life and more life and he is three years old today. It has been a long waiting time for her but she has waited with him for this day and for the promise of green ice cream speaking. She wants so very much for him to say green; green ice cream. Even though he has never said a word, an intelligible word, even Mama . . .

She gazes at him and wonders if he knows the importance of this day for him; for her. He stares back with his large unblinking bulbous eyes; his head oversized is propped up by a cushion.

She had thought to take him out to a shop which sold green ice cream but she did not. On this day she does not want the looks of pity and of contempt; besides going anywhere was an ordeal for him. Noise of any kind made him wail; made that head of his swing until she thought it would become disconnected as she was when the wailing began and never seemed to end until he was taken back home, here.

Simi brings the ice cream from the fridge and scrapes its hardness until it is soft and spoons it into a glass and she marvels at its fresh growth green paleness not so pale.

For three unresponsive years she has repeated the mantra to him every morning and every night before she puts him to bed; she has said-- green ice cream say green ice cream green ice cream.

She sits before him with the glass of green ice cream. She dips a little spoon into the ice cream and tastes it and it is soft on her tongue. Its sweet milky flavour floods the whole of her. She looks at her son. His eyes look past her and she says, "Today is your birthday" she says, "And I'm giving you this special gift of green ice cream. It's more than ice cream my son. It's a promise I made like it seems for ever . . . when I give it to you . . . and I know you can hear me; I know you can understand what I'm saying; when I give it to you please my darling son, please say green ice cream"

She bends forward and attempts to put a spoonful of ice cream on his little jut of red tongue which always and always juts out.

He flinches at the ice cream's coldness. He spits; he opens his mouth wide and bawls and Simi pushes the spoon of ice cream into his mouth. He swallows and he begins to scream loud and louder. And when the tears fall on her face and she feels the wet wetness of them something in her heart breaks into a thousand and one pieces. She knows she is screaming and what will happen when she screams but she screams, "Please, I'm begging you my son. I know you understand how I love you. Please, please take a spoonful of this green ice cream. I know you can't say green ice cream but please...for God's sake, say green ice cream!"

The expected happens. The child defecates and the child urinates and Simi can feel in the whole of her the odour of urine and faeces which run in a streaming stream of filth down and down her son's legs. He is bawling.

She tells him she is sorry. It doesn't matter sweetheart. Nothing matters- she says to him. You are a part of me and I love you so very much and you don't know and never will; will you my son? You will not live for much longer and that doesn't matter too.

She picks him up and cradles him in her arms. But she cannot prevent the tears which flow unchecked down her cheeks. She has been too demanding, too insensitive for a wish a promise made for her and not for him...and her heart breaks again and again and the tears flow; they flow until her face is so wet she feels she has no face left. What could she have been thinking to try to force this child . . . green ice cream ice cream green . . . a promise and a promise only . . .

The face of her and the whole of her are surprised when the child for the first time in his life pulls at her chin and brings her face closer. And with his little tube of red tongue and his oversized head a lolling thing like a swollen pregnant nut is his head; the child holds her face and brings her face closer and closer still and with his little tube of red tongue he licks her face, licks it; licks her face clean.

Salt and Peppers

"And make sure it's secret. No one must know except for the family and except, of course, for the bag of peppers, the hottest ones you can find," said the Minister of Agricultural Affairs to his retainer.

And the retainer, as well as the Minister's servants, wives and children, all smiled knowingly.

The Minister was preparing to visit his English doctor, *oyinbo* friend, secretly that night at a dinner party just for them.

It had to be secret because the Minister had to forgo an important meeting that very night with the President of Nigeria. And if the President got to know that his favourite Minister was abandoning a national meeting of utmost secrecy and importance to have dinner with his *oyinbo* doctor friend he would be more than upset.

The Minister was a cautious man. As for his retainer, he had already anticipated the Minister's need for red hot peppers and held the bag out to him. Inwardly he thanked God that he himself wasn't the Minister.

"Open the bag Retainer and let me see the peppers! And while you're at it take that grin off your face. On no account must you grin and bring me shame at the dinner Retainer" said the Minister looking into the bag. There would be enough peppers. He needed them to smother the taste of his doctor friend's atrocious cooking. It was a shame that she was such a terrible cook. The Minister rubbed his chin meditatively.

The last meal he had had at her house had also taken place during another important meeting with the President which he had also forgone. It had been her birthday, and because she had selflessly given of her medical services to himself and family, the community, he felt it necessary to risk the wrath of the President and attend a small dinner party in her honour. Secretly. At night. She was not only an excellent medical doctor but a woman who really cared, body and soul, for anyone who was sick. That time when his youngest child was on the point of death . . . all the drugs, injections hadn't been able to make her open her eyes. The doctor had spent sleepless nights by the child's bedside, talking to her, holding her hand, persuading her to drink the gruel until, finally, she had recovered her health. The doctor, the woman, was a marvel. He would miss her. She was retiring; leaving Nigeria after having spent more than half her life in the country. It was a shame that she was such a bad cook. She preferred to do her own cooking especially when entertaining friends. And when the watery gravy, the half-cooked chicken, the stringy carrots or anything else she had concocted met the palettes of her guests, none said a word; the Minister himself had passed around secret instructions on the nature of her cooking and had told virtually the entire community to say nothing; just eat the food and say nothing. I don't want my friend to be upset unnecessarily. The Minister did not want to break the heart of one who had for so many years given her whole heart in service, selfless, to others.

And so the more brazen of her guests would simply ask for water on such occasions and gulp it down in glassfuls telling their hostess that drinking so much water while eating aided digestion and that being a doctor she should understand.

The Minister did not care so much for water. But he could withstand the horrible food by chomping red hot peppers which he had at many a dinner party. He sighed. The doctor had said that she was 'doing something special' this evening. And he had enquired, gently, what she would serve; and she told him. A cold avocado soup which she was sure he would like; followed by chicken pie and Brussels sprouts with chestnuts.

Where would she find Brussels sprouts and chestnuts in Nigeria?

Why, in the supermarkets of course. She had beamed. And, she said, the Minister could always spice things up with his peppers. She knew how much he loved hot red peppers. Then she was going to conclude the dinner with ice-cream. She had bought one of those hand- turning ice-cream machines; had bought the ice, cream . . . and well, the Minister, she said, would be pleased. It was an honour that he was coming to grace her table on the eve of her departure from Nigeria when he had lots of important things to attend to.

"Let us proceed," said the Minister to his Retainer who still had that grin on his face. In fact it had become even more pronounced.

The Minister regarded him closcly...

"I'm thinking of making you eat the dinner and saying it's a new custom we have here in Nigeria."

The grin vanished, but remained in abeyance throughout the evening.

The avocado soup was served. The Minister ate rapidly. As soon as he had finished, he clicked his fingers lightly. It was the signal to his Retainer, who stood behind the Minister's chair.

And the retainer presented the bag of red peppers. The Minister sank his teeth into two peppers, chewing and swallowing. When the main course was served his heart and his stomach somersaulted simultaneously. After a few bites of the Brussels sprouts, which had lived in tins for a number of years and were angry about it, the Minister ate three hot red peppers. With the chestnuts it was the same. With the chicken pie, the Minister feeling his stomach and his heart turning, decided to finish the remaining hot red peppers. The chicken, if it could have spoken, would have told him not on any account to eat the pie. It had once been a tender bird at the tender stages of its chicken life but now it had grown old and was somewhat stringy. As for the pastry . . . the Minister made a mental note to look into flour production in his state. He was after all the Minister of Agriculture Affairs and that included the production of wheat. The peppers, hot, wild and fiery in his mouth had made the meal bearable. He could leave his dear friend with a clear conscience. She would never know how really terrible her cooking was, of how he had suffered.

The doctor was looking at him. Having been concentrating on the meal, he had not had much time to engage in conversation.

"Sir, Minister I knew you liked peppers but I had no idea you liked them so much. I see your bag of peppers is finished. I have some more in the kitchen if you like . . ."

The grin, which had been hiding in secret all the while, appeared on the Retainer's face.

"If I'd known," continued the doctor genially, "I would have popped some into the chicken pie. What did you think?

Did you like it Sir?" she asked, her eyes eager.

"Delicious," muttered the Minister.

"Come to think of it, Sir, I haven't seen you eating peppers at any other gathering except in my house . . ."

"Haven't you?" asked the Minister, his tone non-committal.

Thank God the meal was over. But it wasn't. Not quite. Not yet.

The doctor stacked the dishes and murmured.

"Won't be a moment. I'll get the ice-cream. It's home-made. I bought a special machine, not the new fangled type; but the one where you churn the mixture by hand."

The Minister's Retainer still had that grin on his face. He was anxious to see this new development. The bag of hot red peppers had come to an end and he knew that the Minister would not accept the offer of the Doctor's peppers which she said she had in the kitchen. It seemed that his Minister had scored again, another victory in trying to, and succeeding in, getting through the battle of the meal. That was probably why he was the Minister. And that ice-cream. Nothing for the Minister to worry about.

The Retainer had heard of ice-cream. It was a kind of sweet, coldish milky cream thing. Looking at the doctor entering the dining-room and as she served the ice cream in scoopfuls in big glasses, her eyes twinkling the Retainer was pleased that the meal had gone so well. The doctor was bubbling over with talk as she served her dear friend the Minister anticipating the delicious taste of the ice cream and how her dear Minister would enjoy it. Such a wonderful man. So kind. So thoughtful. A little taciturn sometimes, but then Ministers were expected to be aloof, taciturn sometimes. When she sat down at the table she looked at the Minister a smile on her lips and in her eyes. The Minister took up his spoon with a courageous hand. He was on his own. His pepper supply was finished. He wouldn't give offence by asking her for peppers. He was, definitely, on his own. But this was ice cream; there was nothing to worry about.

The doctor's face before him, smiling. And in his mouth a salty taste; making him want to retch. The doctor noting his face. The face of the Minister. The doctor tasting her ice-cream, the ice-cream she had made especially for the Minister and tasting; the doctor tasting a salty liquid texture.

Her face; her life crumbling as she says her voice a moaning sound, "It's got, it's got in it...I don't know how it happened...I...the ice cream's got salt in it and I..." The doctor's face strained, dejected, broken.

"Nonsense, my dear friend! It's delicious. I've never tasted ice cream like this before. May I have another helping please?" says the Minister.

The doctor's face as young as when she first met the Minister and he met her.

And on the Retainer's face a studied gravity. And the beginning of shame and embarrassment and . . . he couldn't have done what the Minister had done with the salt and the peppers . . . he would not have done that . . . couldn't have done that even though the doctor's face is so very heartened, yes heartened and bright and grateful . . . he couldn't have done that. The Retainer forgets to grin and he thinks of the hot bright pain of peppers and the seasoning of salt and of ice cream and of how salt and peppers go together . . . salt and pepper . . . he feels shame and the shame is his alone.

Markets

Ibadan Onion Market

Ibadan means 'by the wayside' in English; but this is no way-siding place. Here onions in majesty rule, make their entrance on naked bare shoulders of men. Peruse carpets of grass from on high. Are laid down with care; sit in their wonder of molten-orbed hauteur, regaled as they are in their silver-veined purples of many-layered robes; their deep rose-pink garments, their round disdain. In-holding their perfumes of scent, these onions with leisure sit behind wall of mountain with rushing earth rushing down in greys of the grace which is calm and calming; lain under this mountain of melody-ing slope of grey muted peace, these onions are not eclipsed.

They are prided-placed and await the bargaining for their onion selves.

Everyone needs them, these onions of onions, skin-silked. They roll to the trees for the bargaining process of onions to start and begin under these trees with their strong sturdy trunks; with their leanings of shade; trees vie with onions; pose, elegant their leaves umbrellad covering faces and heads from the sun; the trees sidle up to benches of wood; discuss patterns of shade. The onions ignore. The process of onion buying is about to begin and the onions are onion-imbued with a haughty disdain as they roll towards benches for the ceremony to begin. Some come trundling on wheel barrows pushed by men. Some balance on heads in laze of round onion.

Children and Humour have come. Children carry trays on their heads and they sell pure water in plastic bags which have to be bitten into in chew of cold plastic and angled at mouth for pure cold pure water to be drunk in this silence of trees with their importance of swish shushing shade. Humour stretches its legs and waits unconscious of time moving time in this marketing of onions of onions here in this onion market, the mountain aback; the day will be long in this roundness of orbed onion grace gilded quest. Onions under the mountain; the damp dew soft earth wet with promise. A mountain behind it. This is no way-siding place.

Marako Market

Prices are high here. Expatriates, wealthied, the moneyed are high here and the sellers know of this highness and have made their stalls along the margined edges of perimetering road and on the left is water and straddled across water is lone boat. Stalls, on the-walk-between-jostle-of-produce-and-crowd-walk-between-pavement; sale of crabs and cold eyed fish from nearby sea plucked. There are pyramids of *garri*, cream, white with an enamel of measuring cup mouth-filled and pyramids of beans brown and black-eyed and the grains of white rice and rice yellow. "Taste fine rice Madam" "Customer, bless me this morning."

They have had to move, get out, quit, to move their stalls. For soldiers have whipped, have burnt their sheds and kicked their stalls down and they are down but not down and they rise up with song and are moved to the beach further up under tarpaulin-like tents under which are tables on which are plantains of green and yellow and yams and fruit stalls loaded with prickly pineapples and oranges green and tangerines. Apples are costly and they are green and red and held on the head.

Women tend their babies which crawl and play in the sand. The children follow customers with their bags.

"Madam make I help you?"

One girl has a baby doll strapped to her back. The Hausa traders with their thin aquiline handsomeness and long white gowns as they sell produce from North with huge sacks of sorrel in dark maroon leaf, dried fruit and spices of nutmeg and cinnamon, beans and peas, peppers red hot and crinkly green peppers and sweet peppers large. These last are expensive and roll around fat, expensively fat. Women over here are selling dried fish which look varnish-dipped and the fish have their tails in their mouths.

"Madam if to say you want buy fish, wash am with soap and water before you cook-am."

Marako Market this is, and you pay to enter if you go by car. Not too much.

"Thank you Madam. How is your family? And how are the children?"

There is a row of meat sellers, their coats of white smeared by animal blood, and on the table hunks of fresh meat. Goat meat and beef. They chop up the meat into cubes of meat and you stand back from this chopping of meat. "Madam I give you good price." The housewives browse. Choose. Argue. Debate on freshness, quality, and the market listens, comfort in it that new supplies have been brought by lorries and this is the market, new market of

Marako after the beating and the flailing of whips of policemen and soldiers who said:

"You were warned!"

"You were told!"

"We have to beautify this place!"

"But how will our customers be able to get to New Marako market if there is a fuel shortage?"

Old Marako market was by the petrol station, judiciously positioned. A man gets out of his car. He has directed the cars which are angry and honking.

"Madam I go give you good price if say you fit jump queue."

The market folk have jumped queue and driven home, walked and are now in new market. New market old.

Oyinbo Market/Yaba Market

Oyinbo market near Oyinbo bus stop, where the yellows of taxis and *molues* and *danfos* compete with the yellows of oranges and *agbalumos* sold under faded umbrellas, some striped. A man walks by; across his shoulders a length of pole from which hang shirts of white, blue and gray—men's shirts which he sells to those who want shirts and to those who do not. On the way to market as market hawkers, outlawed, wait to sell newspapers, international magazines like *Newsweek, Vogue, Cosmopolitan* and Nigerian magazines and cotton-wool, and clocks with their ticks and calendars and carvings and small transistor radios and booklets of *Daily Bread*, and dictionaries and Bibles and Korans and calculators, and sweet smelling soap and games of Scrabble and knitted booties for a child of winter born winter though there is no winter; and the ever-present packages of pure water and soft drinks to cool you down in the heat of the wait because further up the road two men have not seen each other since yesterday and have stopped the traffic so that they can exchange greetings.

Another market on the way to market and Yaba indoor and outdoor market. Indoored like *Aladdin's* cave bathed and bottled in luminous electric bulb shine. No windows.

"If I'm going to buy this cloth I'll have to see it properly."

"Let us go for outside Madam."

Outside at the entrance, hairdressers accosting customers.

"You want perm?"

"You want geri curl?"

"Janet Jackson?"

"Shade Adu hairstyle?"

"Bob Marley?"

And then the stalls which sell hair for braiding, extensions and plaits black and brown, blonde and fiery red hair in plastic bags strung up and oils and hairgrips and brushes for hair and combs. Posters of different hairstyles with women smiling in the pictures and coiffed. You are led to Janet Jackson and guided through a network of paths past a man who is being shaved while his companion, his leg thrust out, is having his toe nails clipped; past a bread seller so in love with her bread that she eats it and cats it; and you are led through market corridors, market paths and seated in a cubicle and the hairdresser begins with your hair. A dirty family of goats wanders in. They want to have their hair done. But the hairdresser has no time. A sign. DO NOT URINATE HERE. A man carefully stares at the sign. Urinates, luxuriating in relief. There is a woman who has bundles of chewing sticks bound by rubber bands on the top of her head. She says the chewing sticks are medicinal. You can use them for brushing your teeth and they will prevent your teeth from decaying. She leaves because "the breeze has stolen her temperature."

Outside of the market *okadas* loiter and pose with their motor bike charges. They are hip in dark sunglasses and some sleep on their bikes to ensure not missing any customers. Even though they don't have to. Even though they need not. Signs. Everywhere. Allah is the greatest. Merciful and beautiful. In God we Trust. Honesty. Love is life. The triangular sloping slide of rice, garri, flour.

Beside this stall people are standing. They shiver and drink cups of a brown liquid in which slices of pineapple slices and oranges and spices swim. Drink and your malaria will go. More signs. You can buy them and stick them on your car or on your wall at home. Allah the munificent. Jesus is Lord. The sound of drumming overpowers Dolly Parton and Michael Jackson. They are holding a fellowship. Benches are drawn into the narrow market corridors of life and there is a singing of choruses and a tailor is speaking. He has been sewing at his machine, pedalling the pedals and giving his material to his assistants to cut and to sew into fine garments and he has stopped his pedalling. And to the customers, the sellers of vegetables, garri and meat and material and clocks, it is time to stop and it is time to rejoice in this joy and pain and joy of living and rejoice in this market. These markets.

Rejoice.

Printed in the United States
By Bookmasters